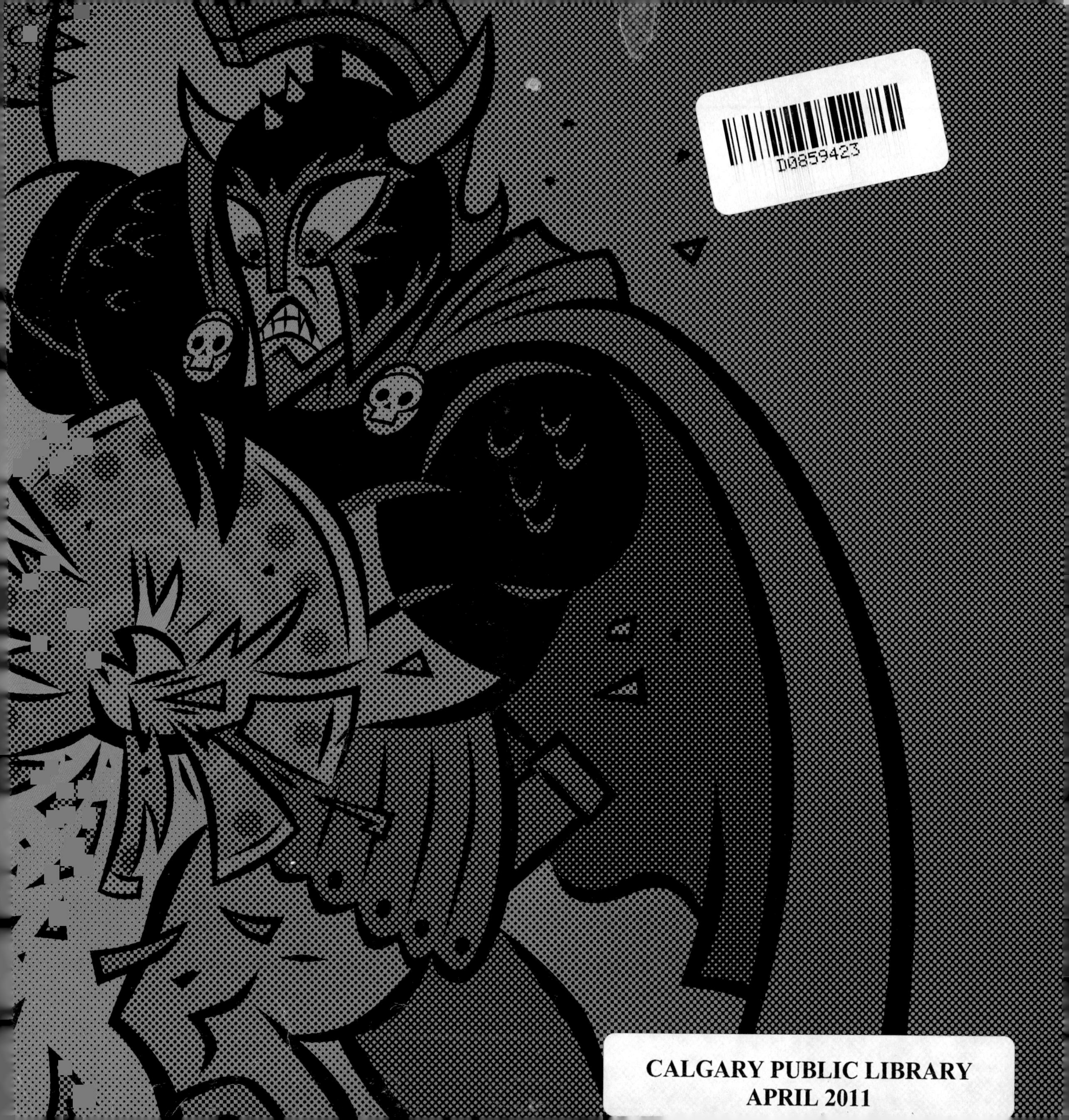

Dedicated to William Moulton Marston,
Harry Peter, and all the inspirational writers and artists through the ages
who have kept Wonder Woman timeless.

And to Lynda Carter for so graciously bringing the Amazon Princess to life and keeping
our family glued to the TV set every Wednesday night.

And most importantly, to my princesses and wonderful daughters, Bella & Sofia.

VIKING
Published by Penguin Group
Penguin Young Readers Group, 345 Hudson Street, New York, New York 10014, U.S.A.
Penguin Group (Canada), 90 Eglinton Avenue East, Suite 700, Toronto, Ontario, Canada M4P 2Y3
(a division of Pearson Penguin Canada Inc.)

Penguin Books Ltd, Registered Offices: 80 Strand, London WC2R 0RL, England

First published in 2011 by Viking, a division of Penguin Young Readers Group

1 3 5 7 9 10 8 6 4 2

www.dccomics.com
Text and illustrations by Ralph Cosentino

LIBRARY OF CONGRESS CATALOGING-IN-PUBLICATION DATA
Cosentino, Ralph.
Wonder Woman / written and illustrated by Ralph Cosentino.
p. cm.
"Wonder Woman created by William Moulton Marston."
Summary: Wonder Woman tells how she came to be the protector of humankind, who her enemies are, and how she keeps her identity secret.
ISBN 978-0-670-06256-0 (hardcover : alk. paper)
1. Wonder Woman (Fictitious character)—Juvenile fiction. [1. Wonder Woman (Fictitious character)—Fiction. 2. Superheroes—Fiction. 3.Amazons—Fiction.] I. Marston, William Moulton, 1893–1947. II. Title.
PZ7.C81855Won 2011 [E]—dc22 2010024540

Manufactured in China **Book design by Ralph Cosentino** Set in Anime Ace

WONDER WOMAN™

THE STORY OF THE AMAZON PRINCESS

WRITTEN & ILLUSTRATED BY
RALPH COSENTINO

VIKING

WONDER WOMAN CREATED BY WILLIAM MOULTON MARSTON

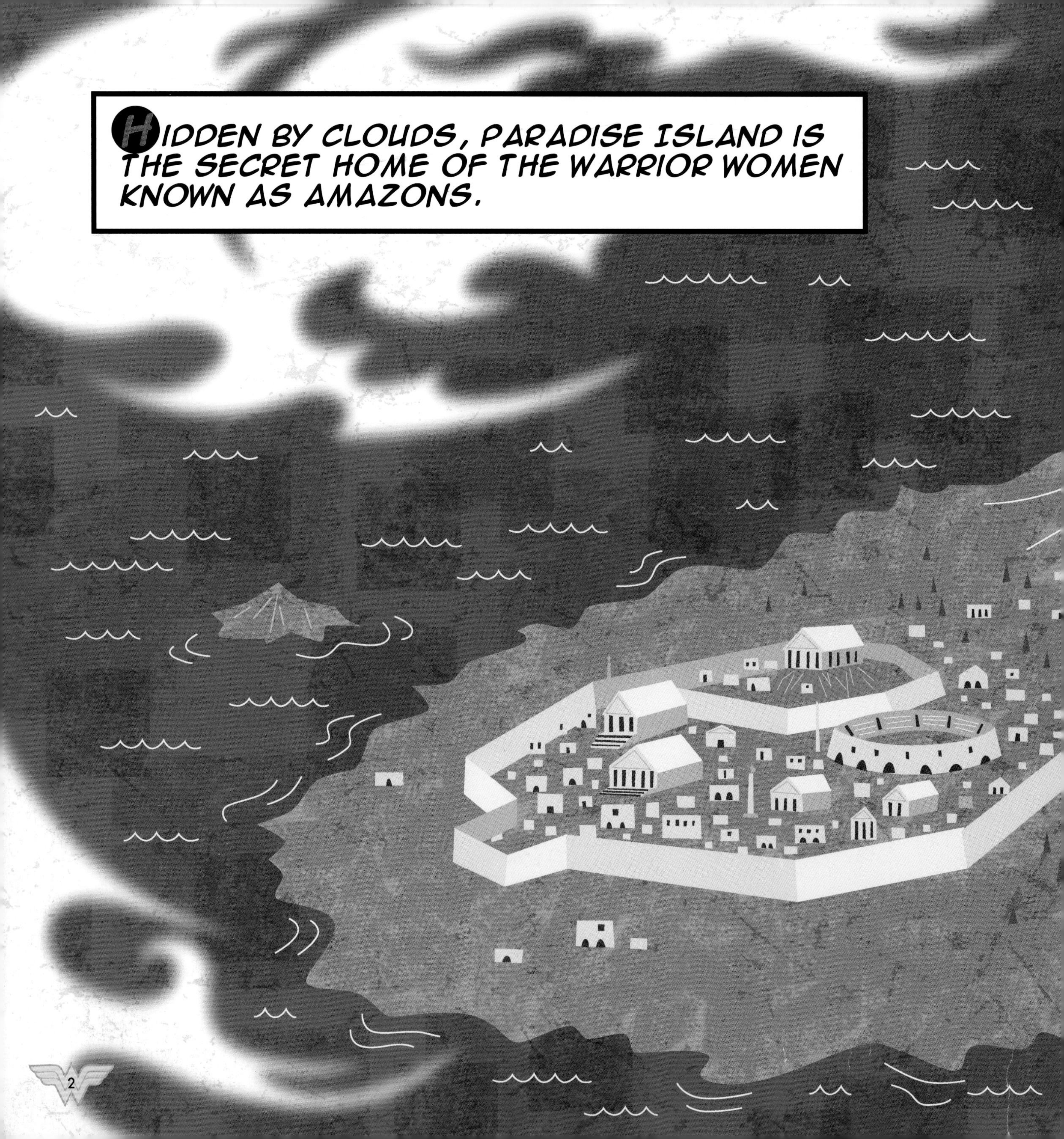
HIDDEN BY CLOUDS, PARADISE ISLAND IS THE SECRET HOME OF THE WARRIOR WOMEN KNOWN AS AMAZONS.

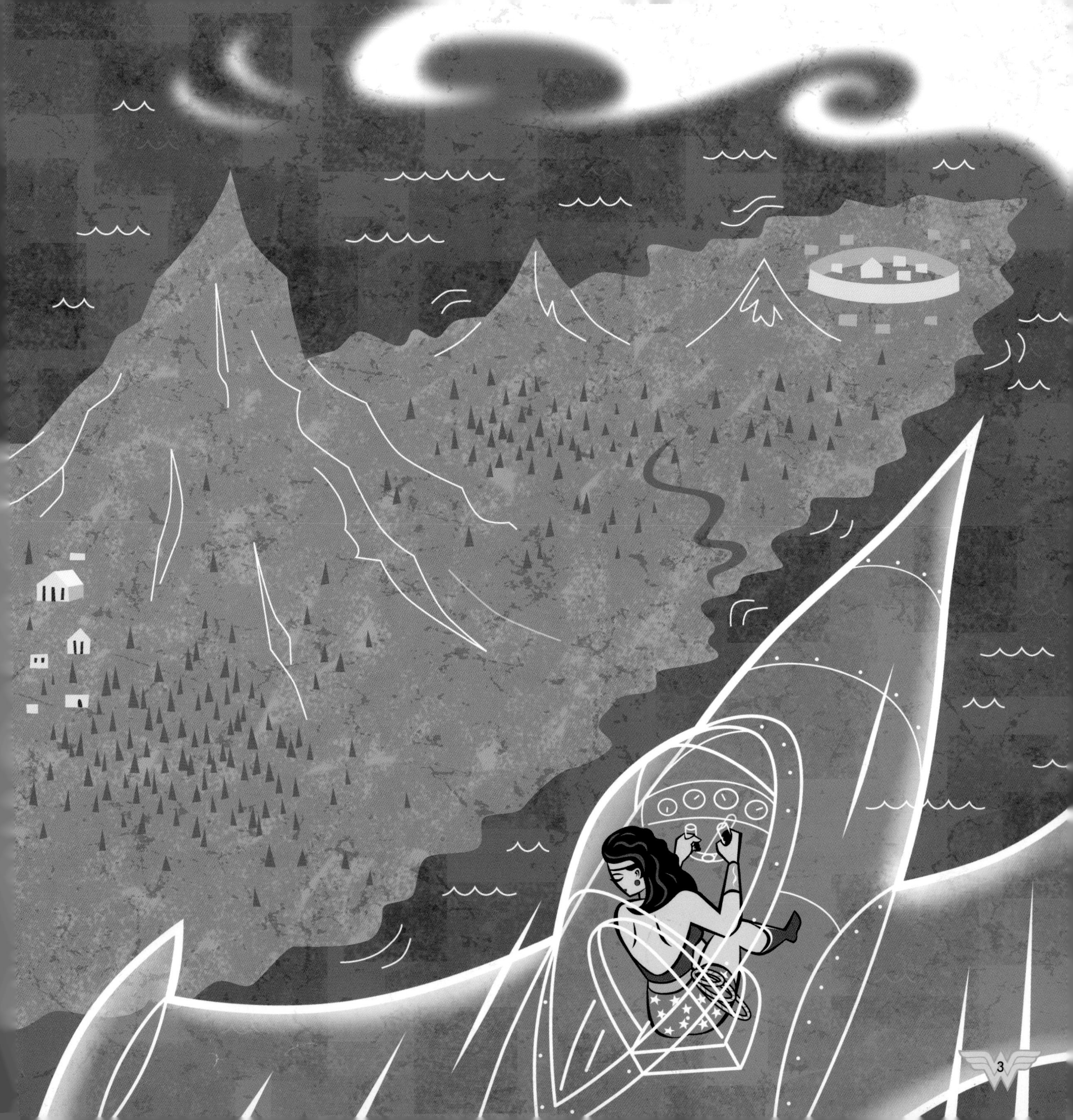

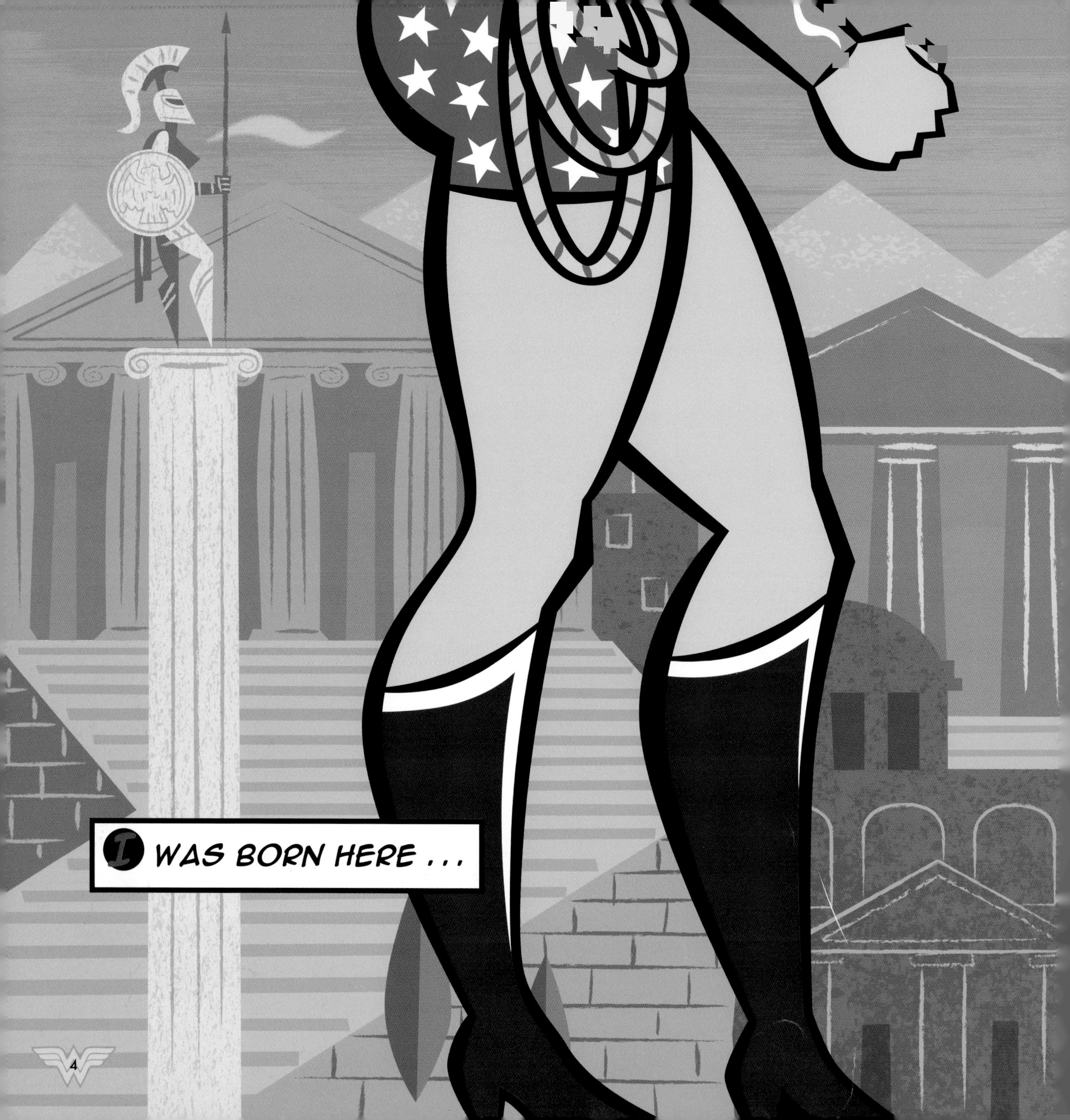
I WAS BORN HERE . . .

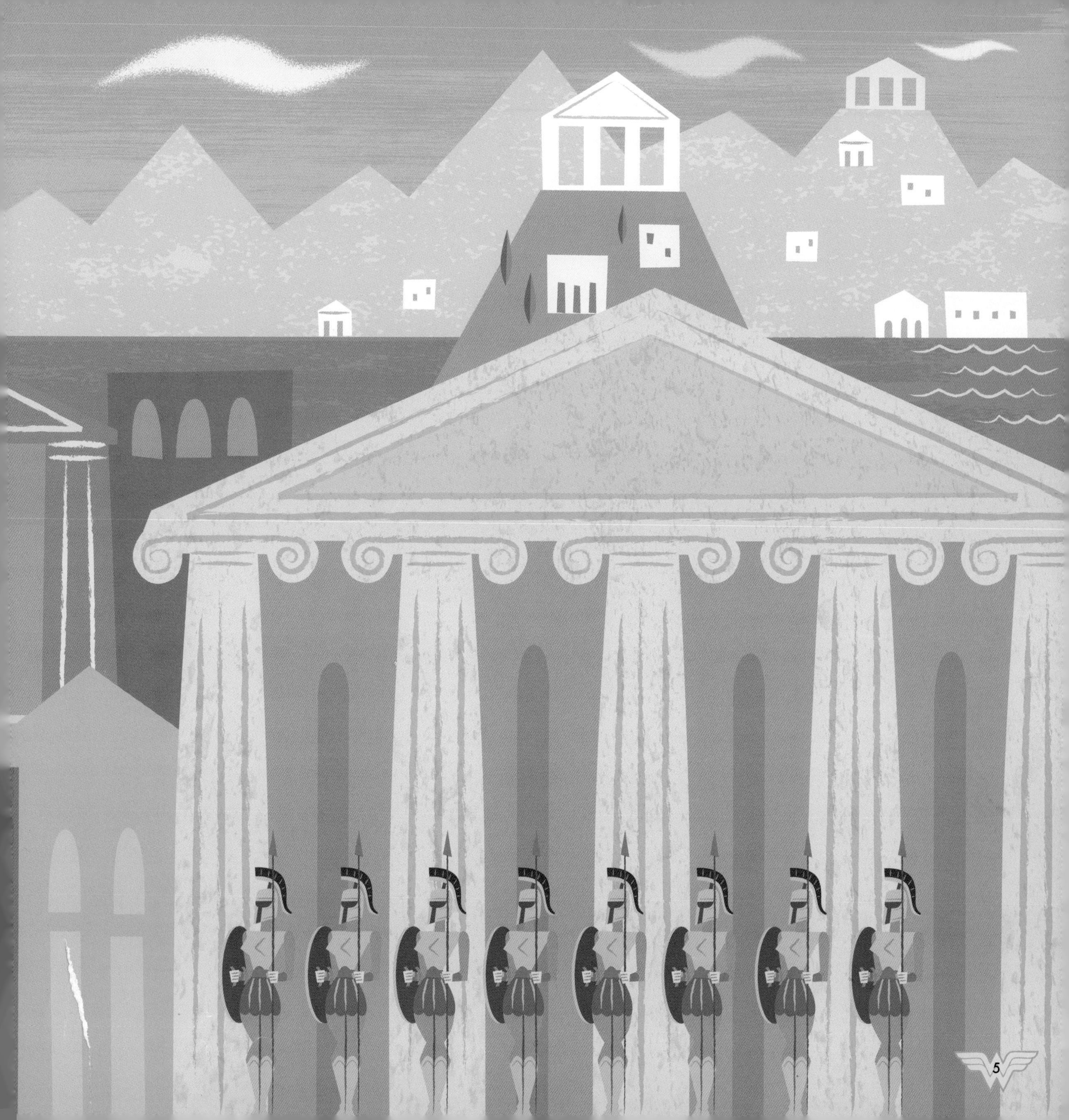

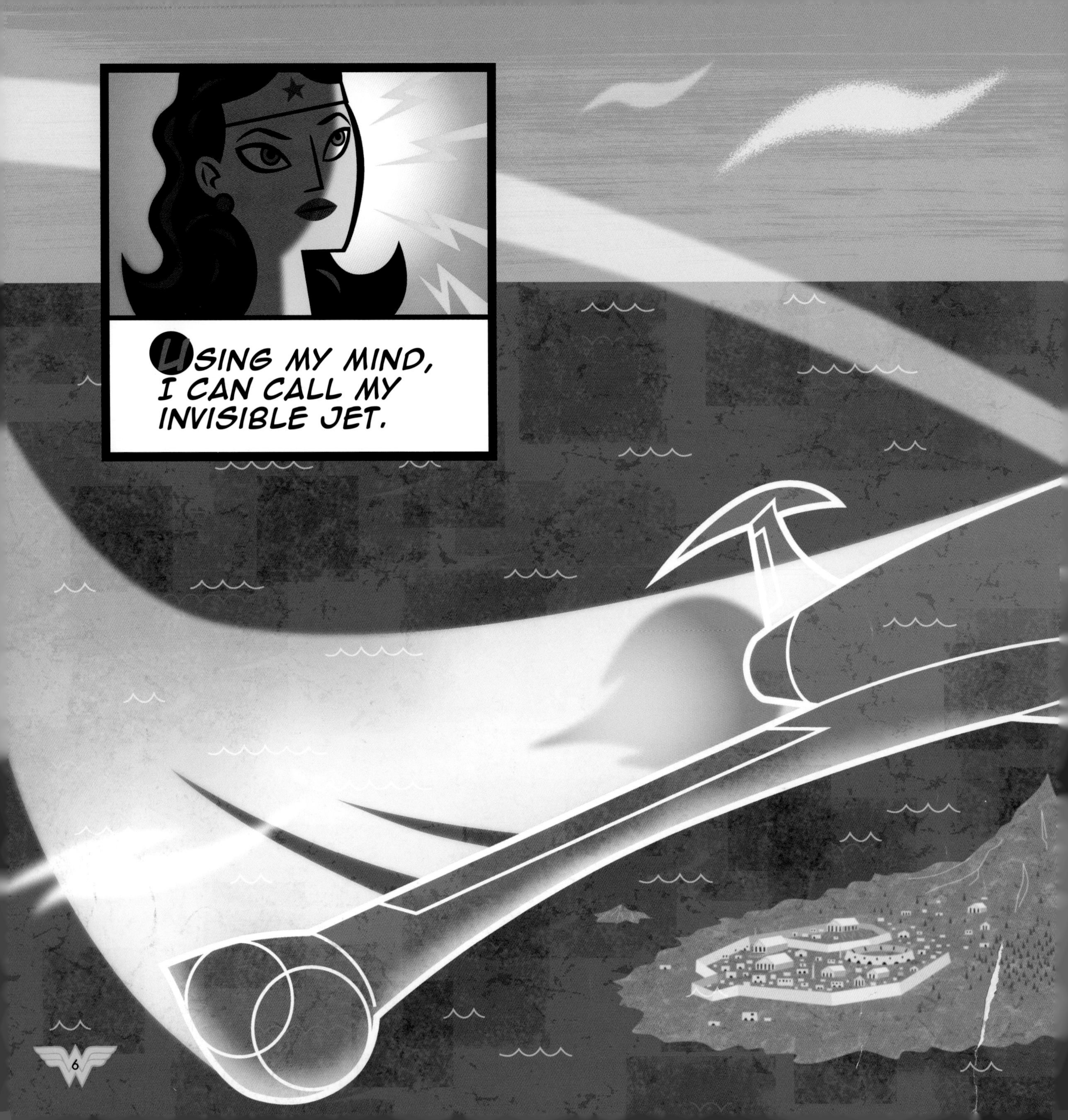
USING MY MIND, I CAN CALL MY INVISIBLE JET.

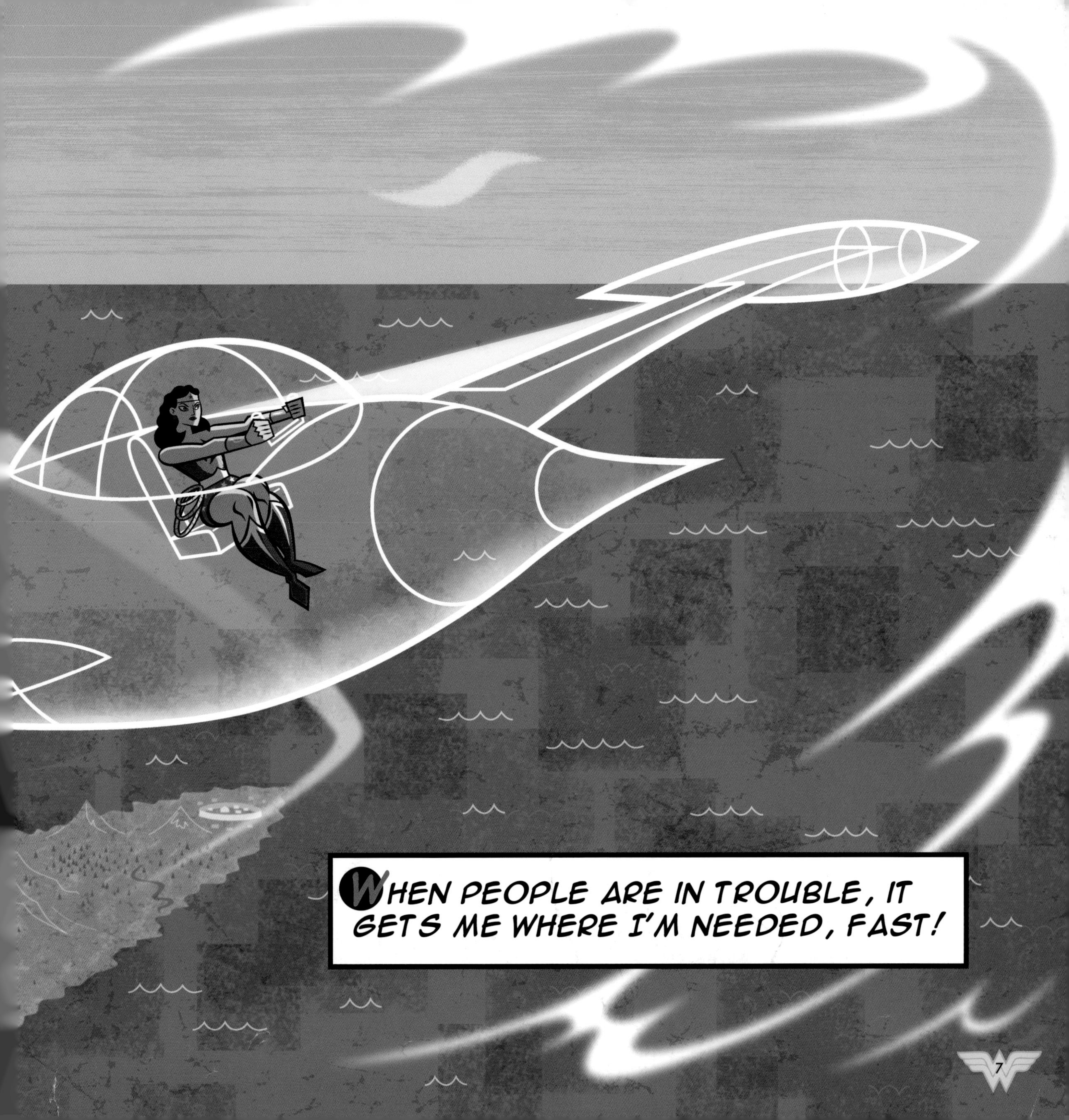
WHEN PEOPLE ARE IN TROUBLE, IT GETS ME WHERE I'M NEEDED, FAST!

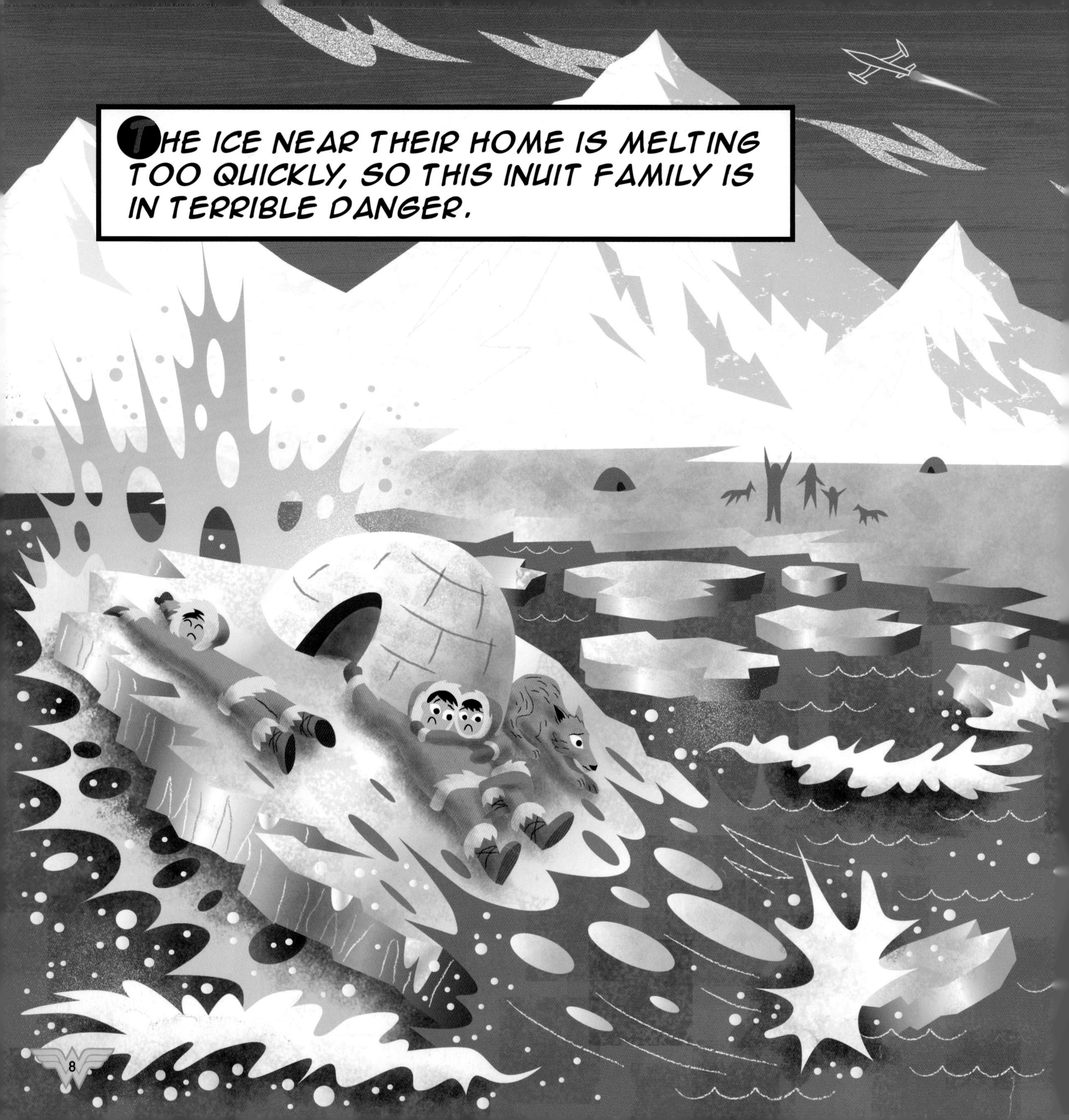
THE ICE NEAR THEIR HOME IS MELTING TOO QUICKLY, SO THIS INUIT FAMILY IS IN TERRIBLE DANGER.

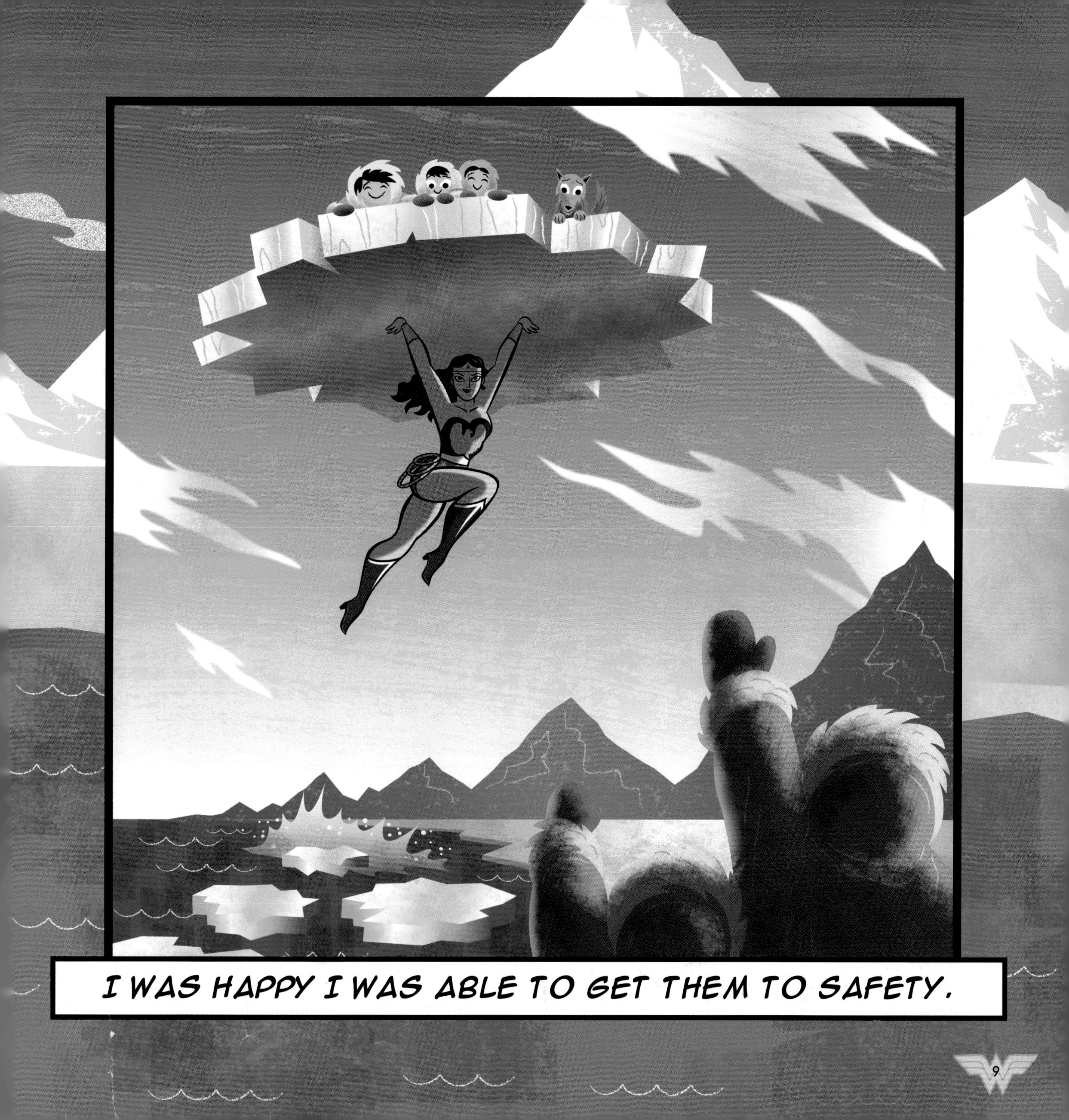
I WAS HAPPY I WAS ABLE TO GET THEM TO SAFETY.

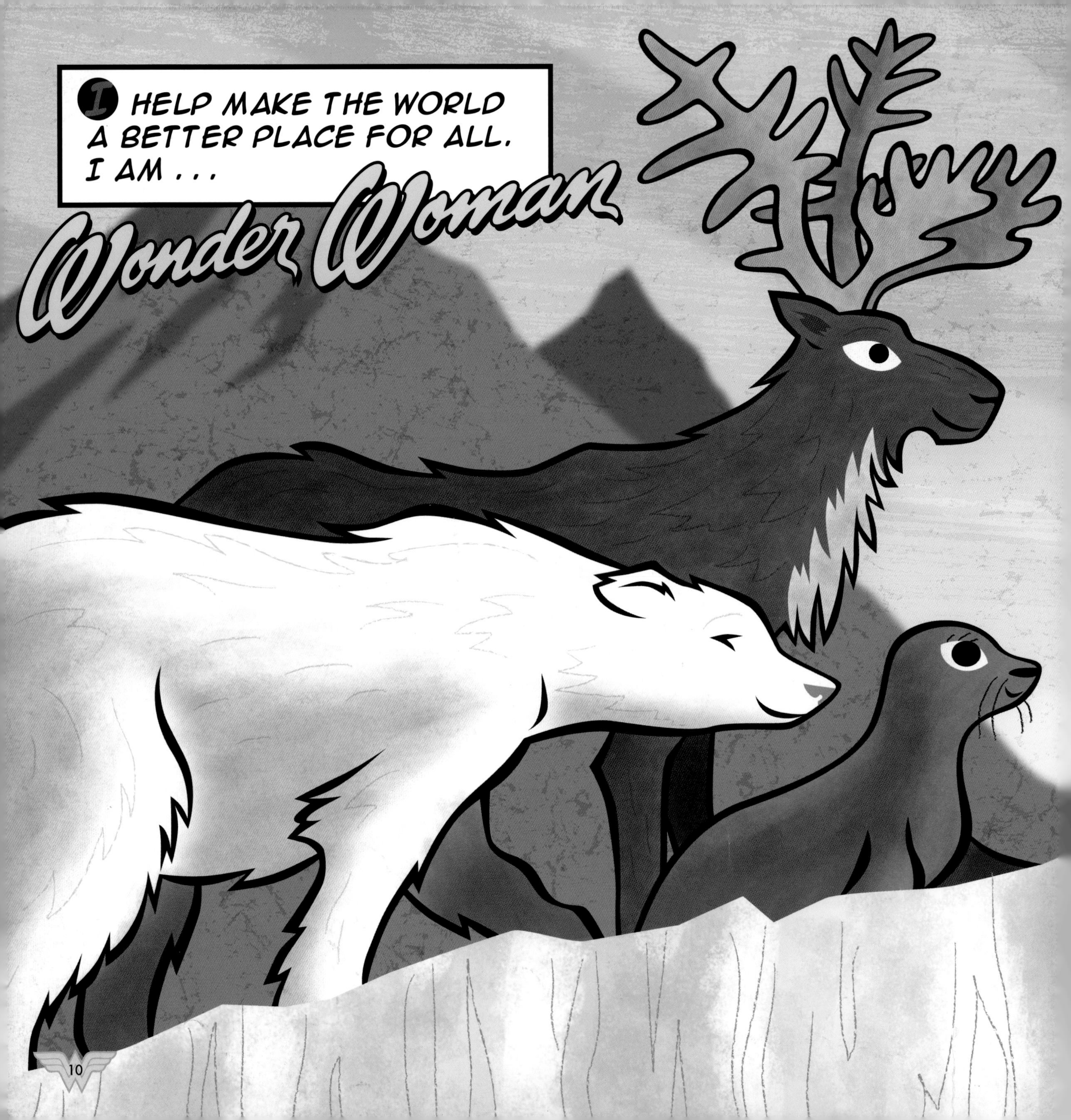
I HELP MAKE THE WORLD A BETTER PLACE FOR ALL. I AM . . .
Wonder Woman

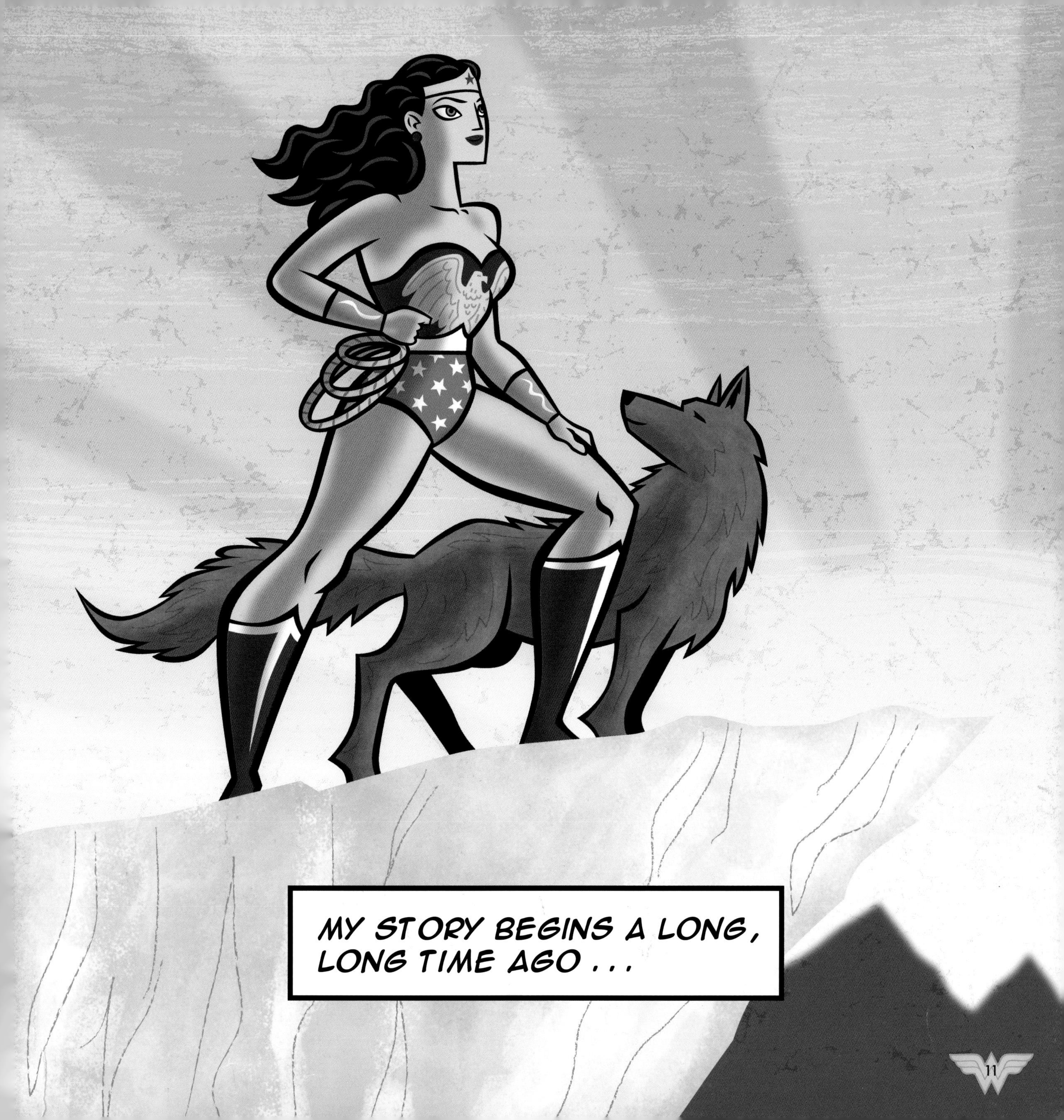
MY STORY BEGINS A LONG, LONG TIME AGO . . .

THE GREEK GODS LIVED HIGH IN THE SKY ON MOUNT OLYMPUS. TO BRING GLORY AND PEACE TO EARTH, THEY CREATED THE MIGHTY AMAZON WOMEN. THE GODS ALSO MADE PARADISE ISLAND.

THE AMAZON QUEEN HIPPOLYTA WANTED A DAUGHTER, SO THE GREEK GODS TOLD HER TO MOLD A BABY OUT OF CLAY. THEY BROUGHT ME TO LIFE AND GAVE ME THEIR SPECIAL STRENGTHS.

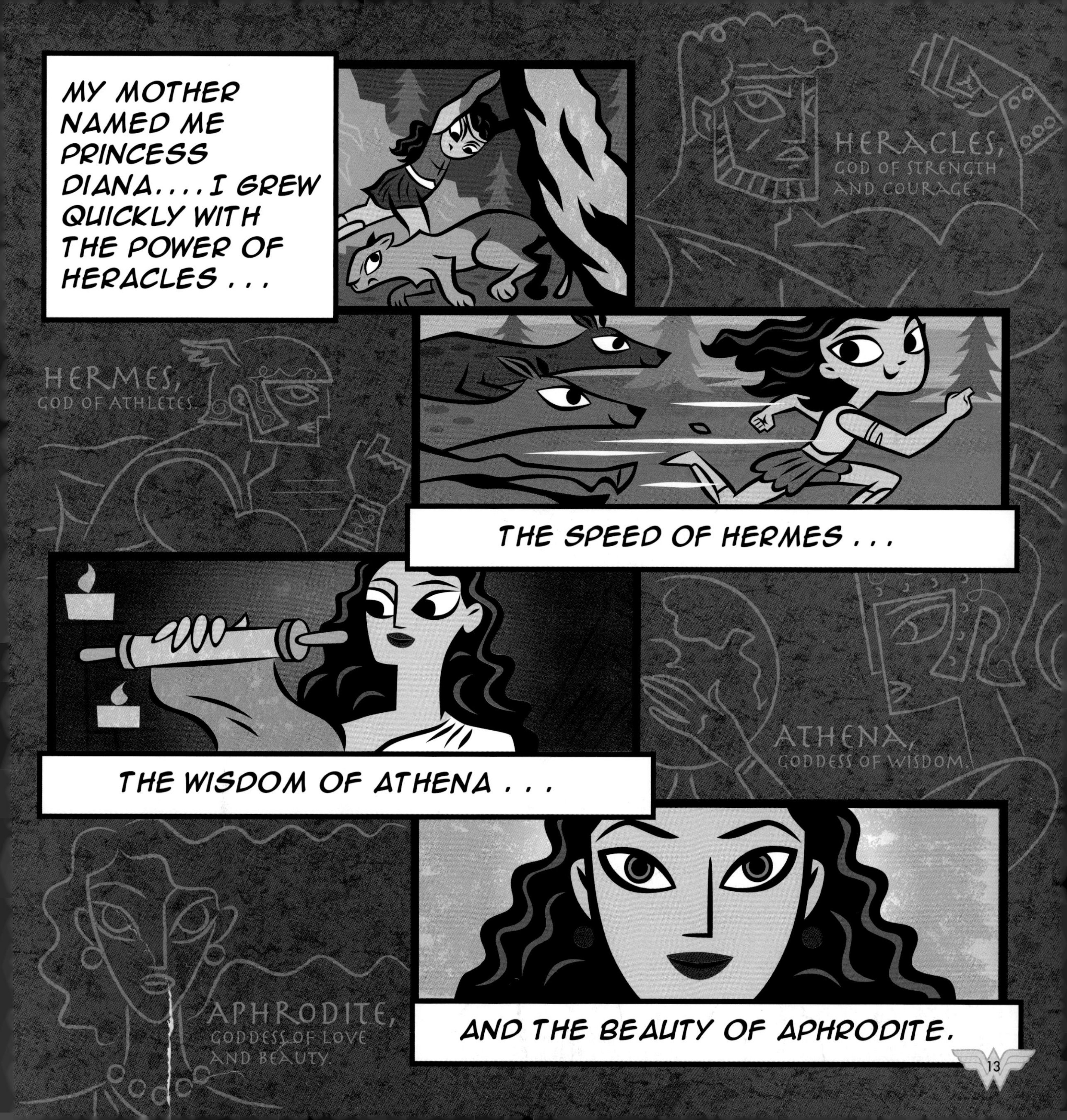
MY MOTHER NAMED ME PRINCESS DIANA. . . . I GREW QUICKLY WITH THE POWER OF HERACLES . . .
HERACLES,
GOD OF STRENGTH AND COURAGE.
HERMES,
GOD OF ATHLETES.
THE SPEED OF HERMES . . .
THE WISDOM OF ATHENA . . .
ATHENA,
GODDESS OF WISDOM.
APHRODITE,
GODDESS OF LOVE AND BEAUTY.
AND THE BEAUTY OF APHRODITE.

BY THE TIME I WAS A YOUNG WOMAN, I HAD BECOME ONE OF THE BEST ATHLETES ON PARADISE ISLAND. BUT THAT WAS SOON PUT TO THE TEST. ARES, THE GOD OF WAR, DECIDED HE WANTED TO RULE THE WORLD.

ZEUS, KING OF THE GODS, PROTECTED THE AMAZONS. BUT HE ASKED THEM TO HOLD A CONTEST AND CHOOSE A WINNER TO DEFEND THE REST OF MANKIND FROM ARES.

MY MOTHER, THE AMAZON QUEEN, KNEW IF I WON I WOULD HAVE TO LEAVE THE ISLAND. SHE DID NOT WANT ME TO GO, SO SHE WOULDN'T ALLOW ME TO ENTER THE CONTEST. WITH THE HELP OF A MASK, I SECRETLY DID.

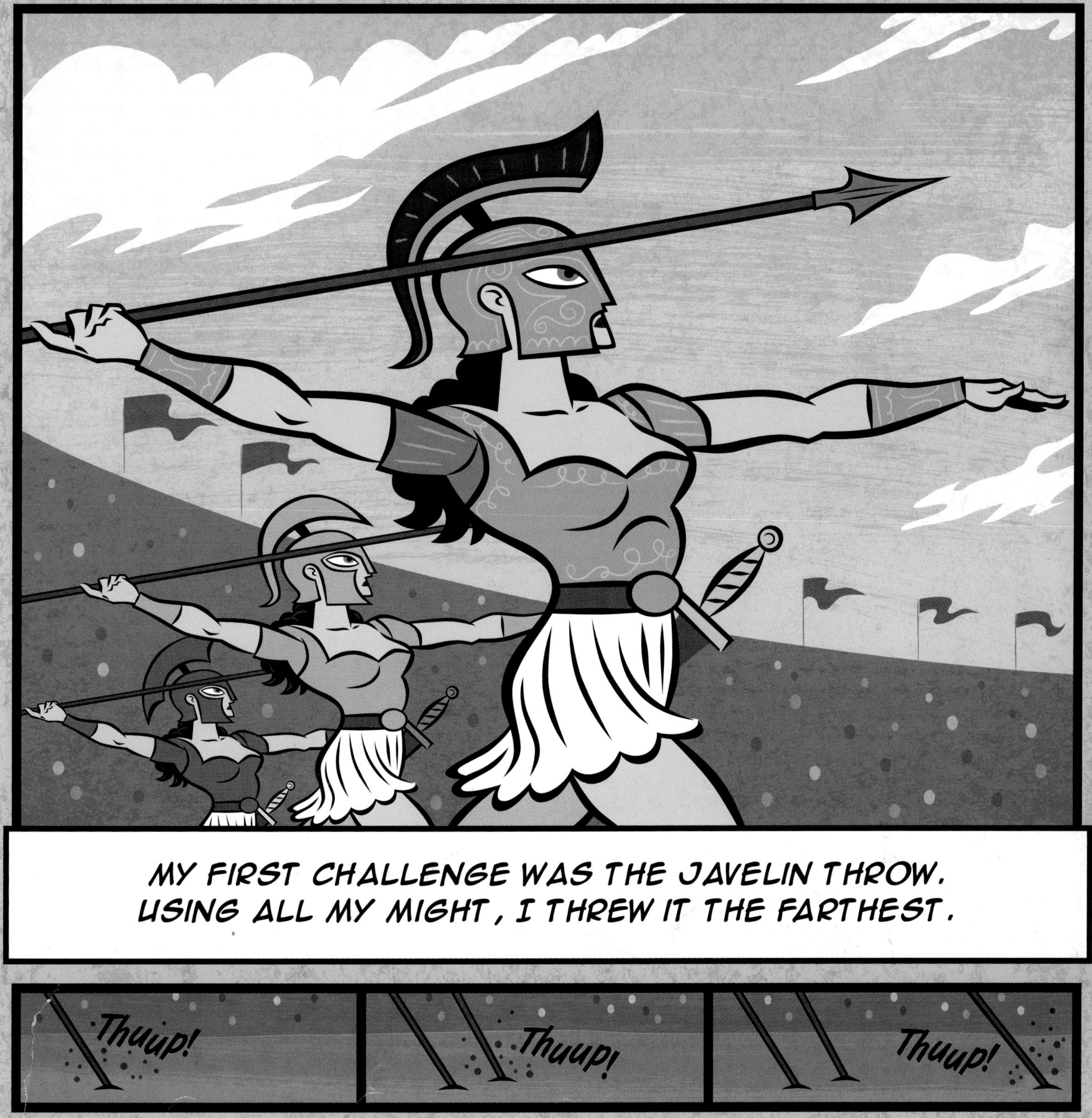
MY FIRST CHALLENGE WAS THE JAVELIN THROW. USING ALL MY MIGHT, I THREW IT THE FARTHEST.
Thuup!
Thuup!
Thuup!

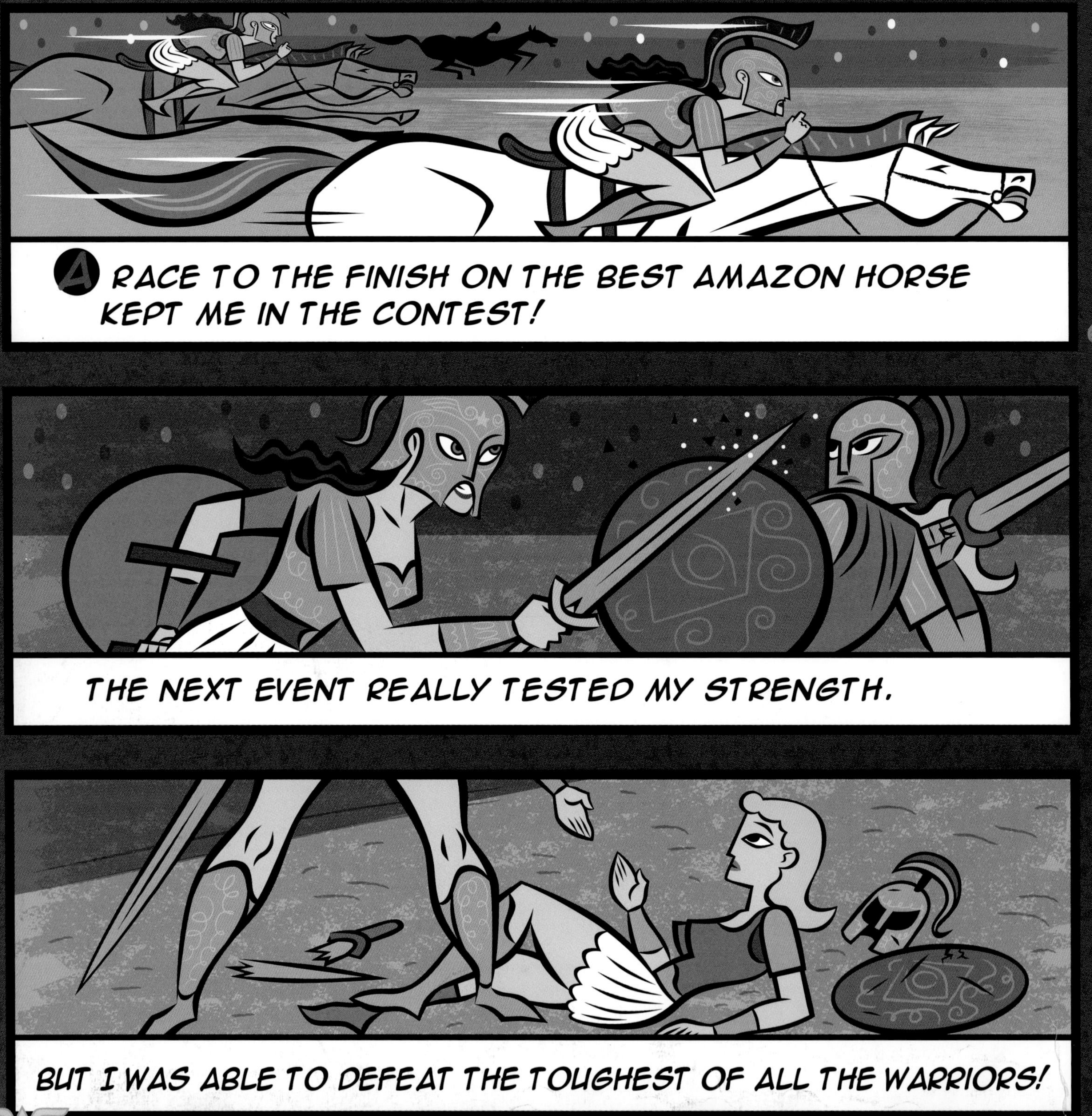
A RACE TO THE FINISH ON THE BEST AMAZON HORSE KEPT ME IN THE CONTEST!
THE NEXT EVENT REALLY TESTED MY STRENGTH.
BUT I WAS ABLE TO DEFEAT THE TOUGHEST OF ALL THE WARRIORS!

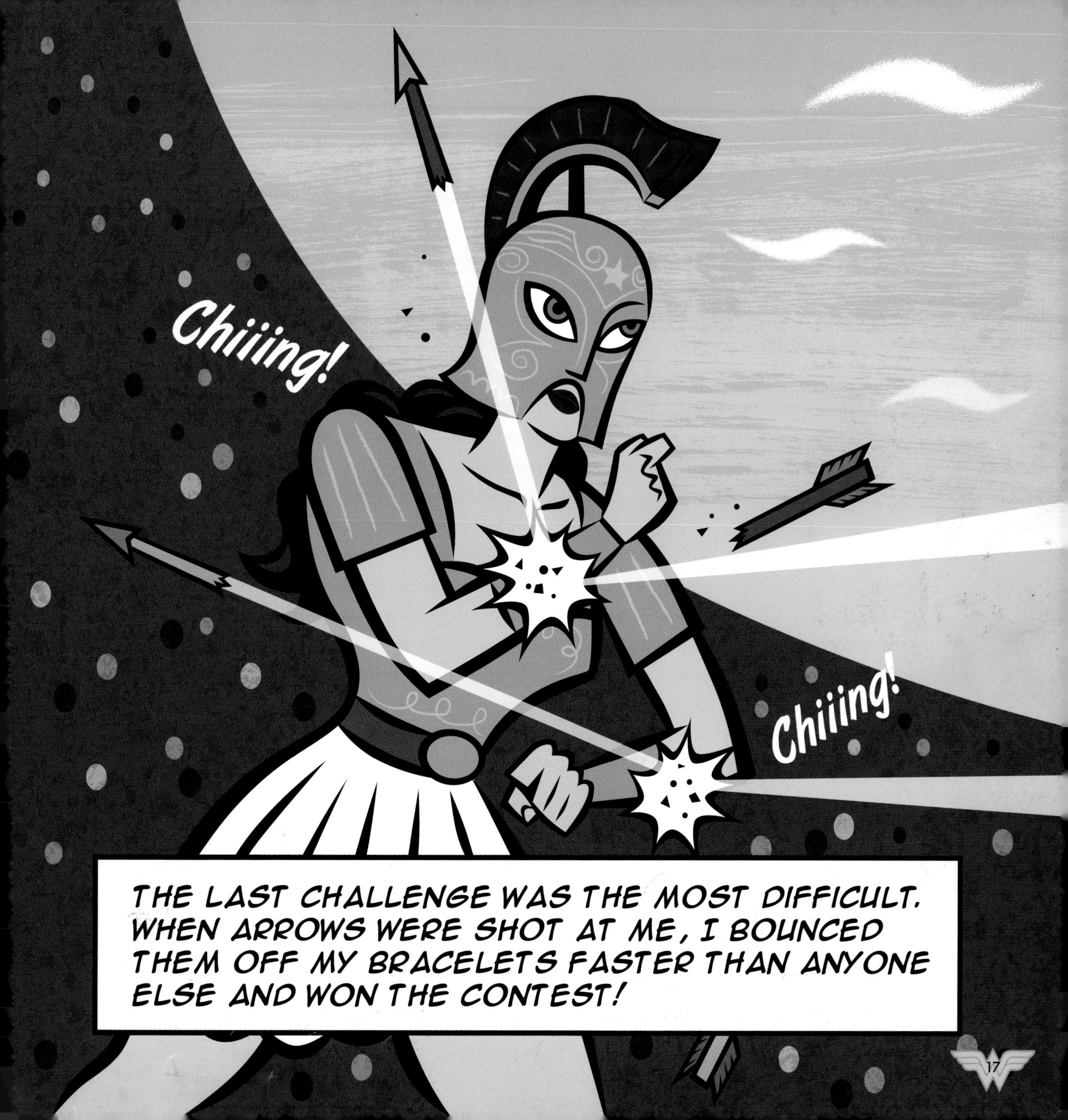
Chiiing!
Chiiing!
THE LAST CHALLENGE WAS THE MOST DIFFICULT. WHEN ARROWS WERE SHOT AT ME, I BOUNCED THEM OFF MY BRACELETS FASTER THAN ANYONE ELSE AND WON THE CONTEST!

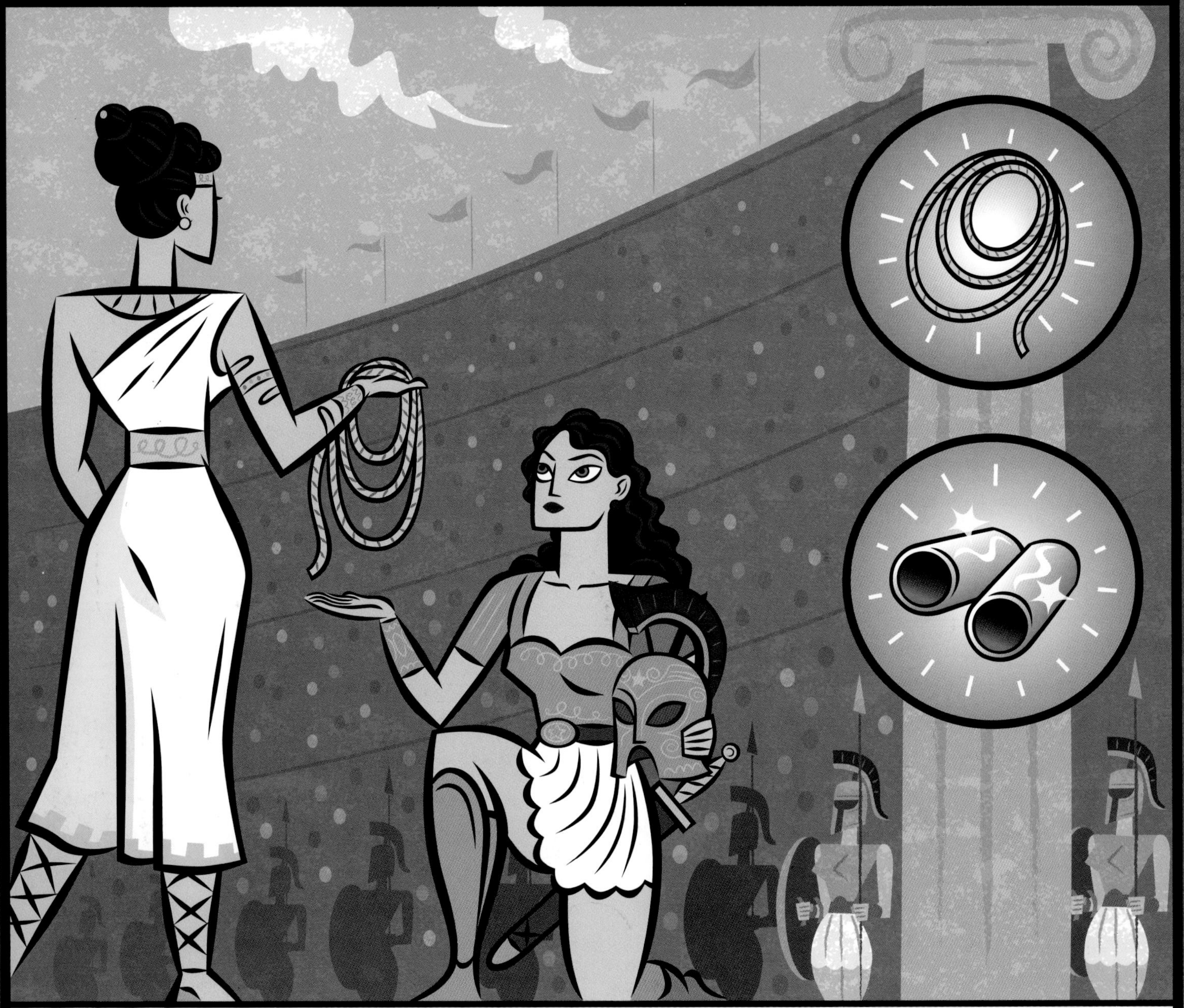

MY MOTHER WAS SHOCKED THAT I WAS THE WINNER, BUT SHE WAS PROUD, TOO. SHE AWARDED ME A SPECIAL COSTUME, UNBREAKABLE SILVER BRACELETS, AND A GOLDEN LASSO OF TRUTH TO BETTER FIGHT ARES.

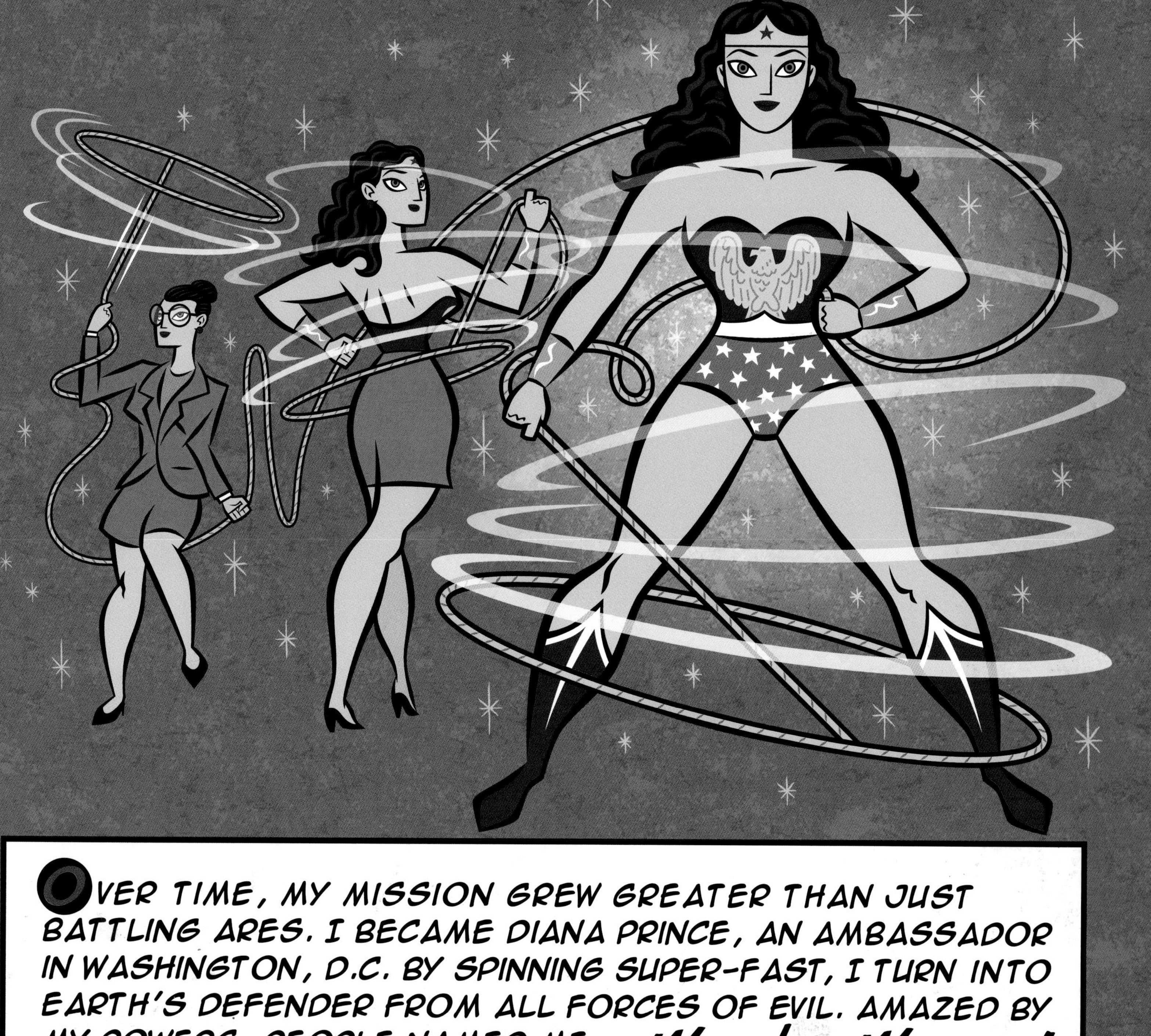

OVER TIME, MY MISSION GREW GREATER THAN JUST BATTLING ARES. I BECAME DIANA PRINCE, AN AMBASSADOR IN WASHINGTON, D.C. BY SPINNING SUPER-FAST, I TURN INTO EARTH'S DEFENDER FROM ALL FORCES OF EVIL. AMAZED BY MY POWERS, PEOPLE NAMED ME . . . **Wonder Woman!**

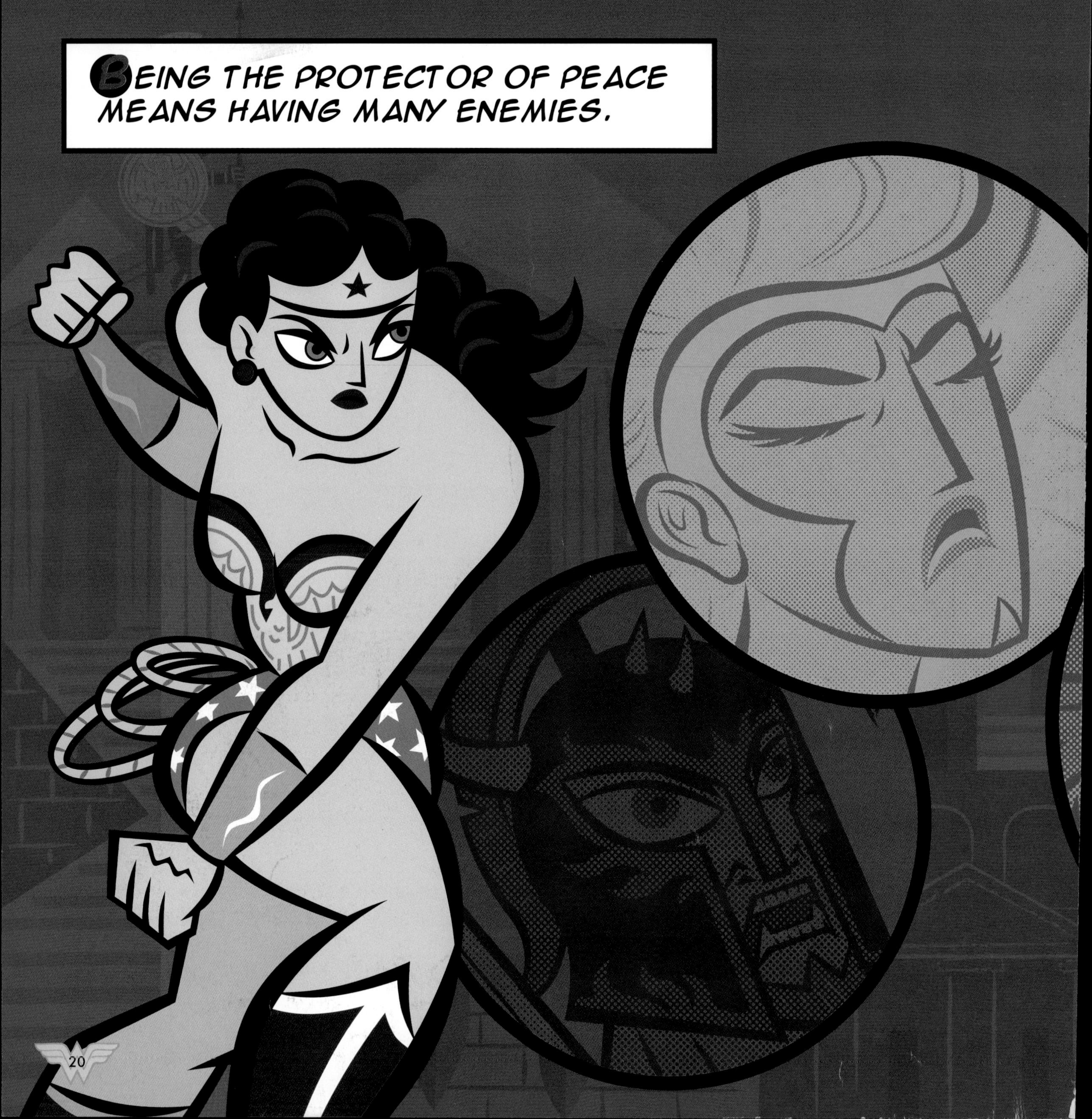
BEING THE PROTECTOR OF PEACE MEANS HAVING MANY ENEMIES.

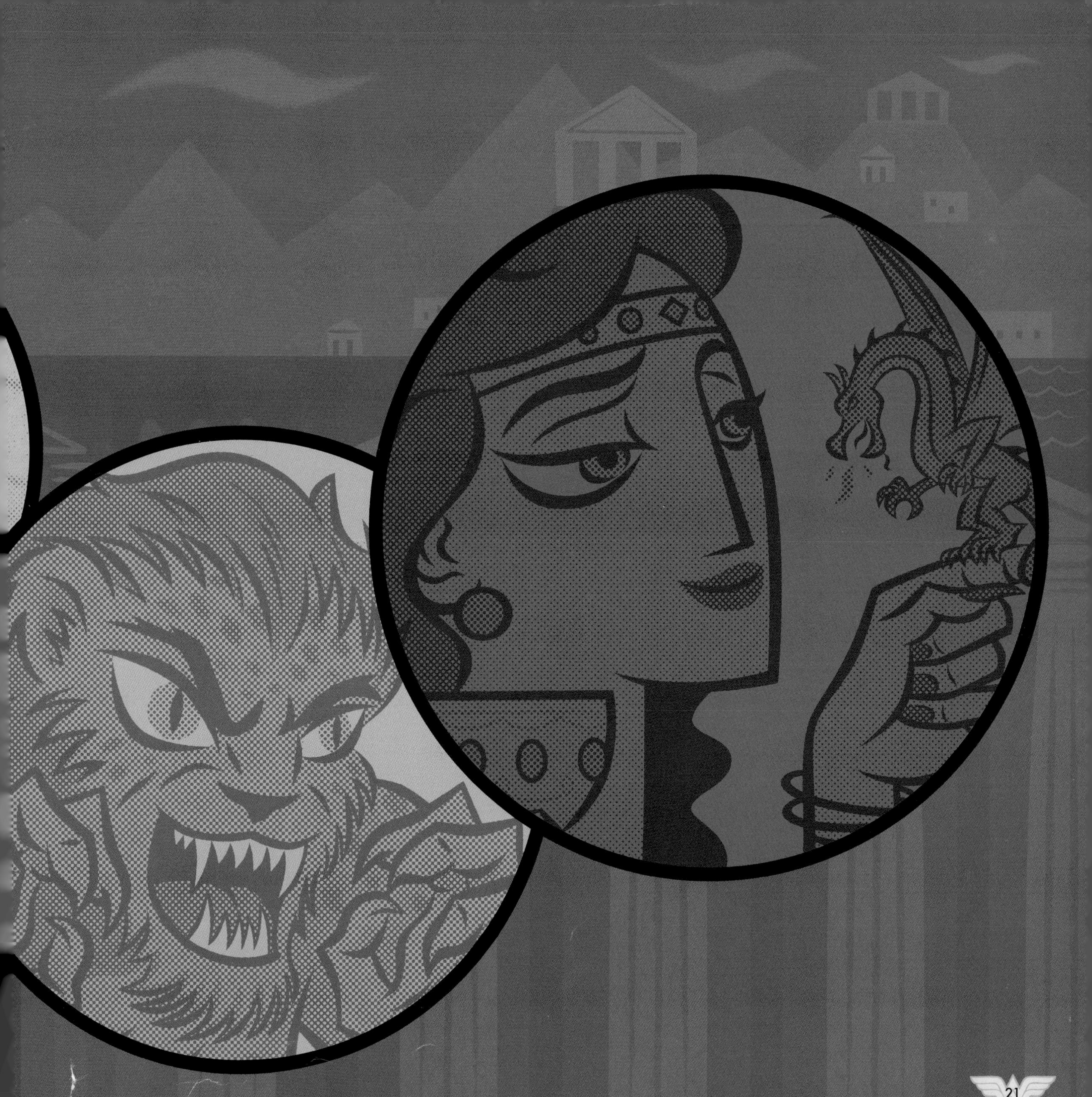

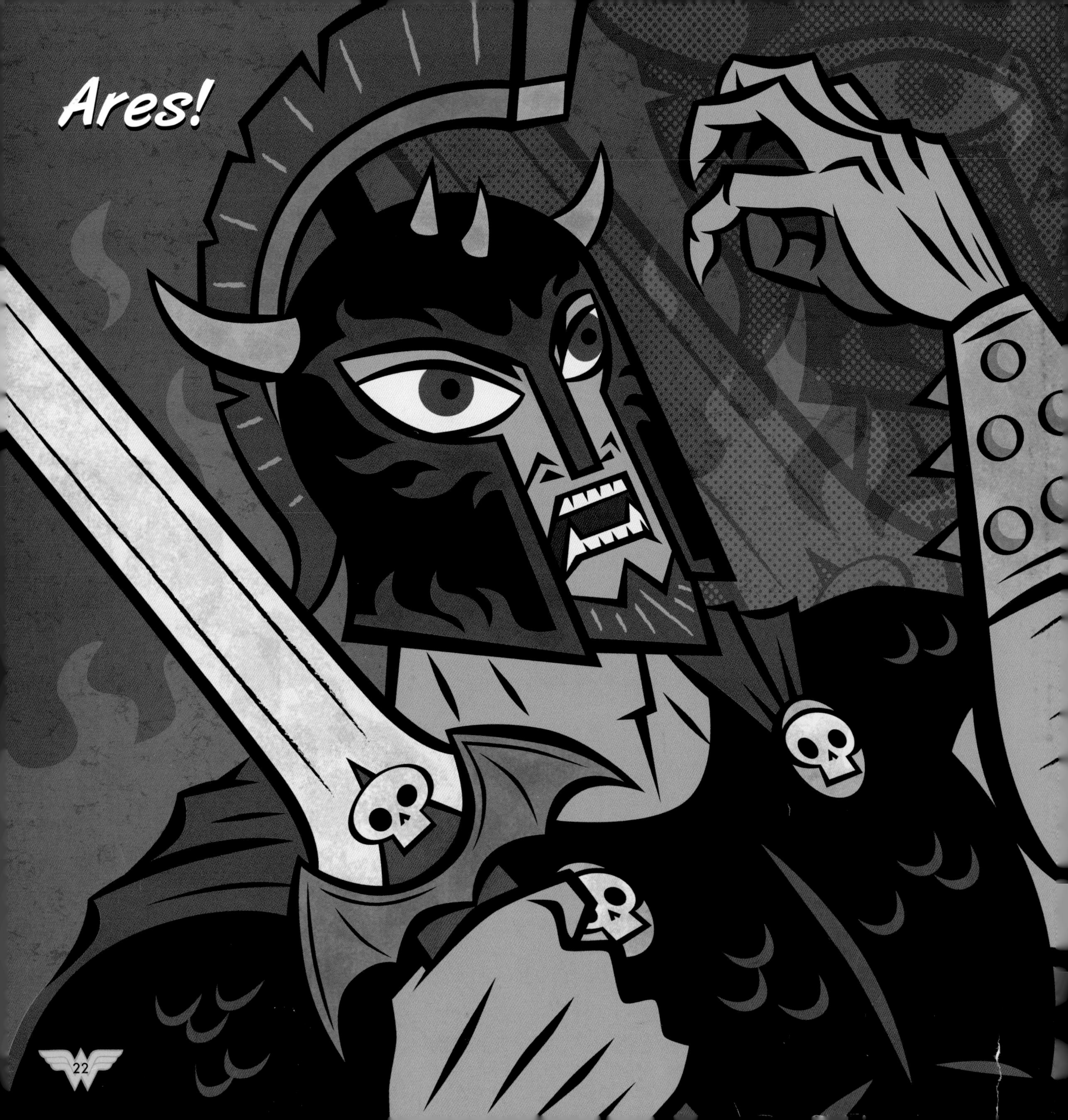
Ares!

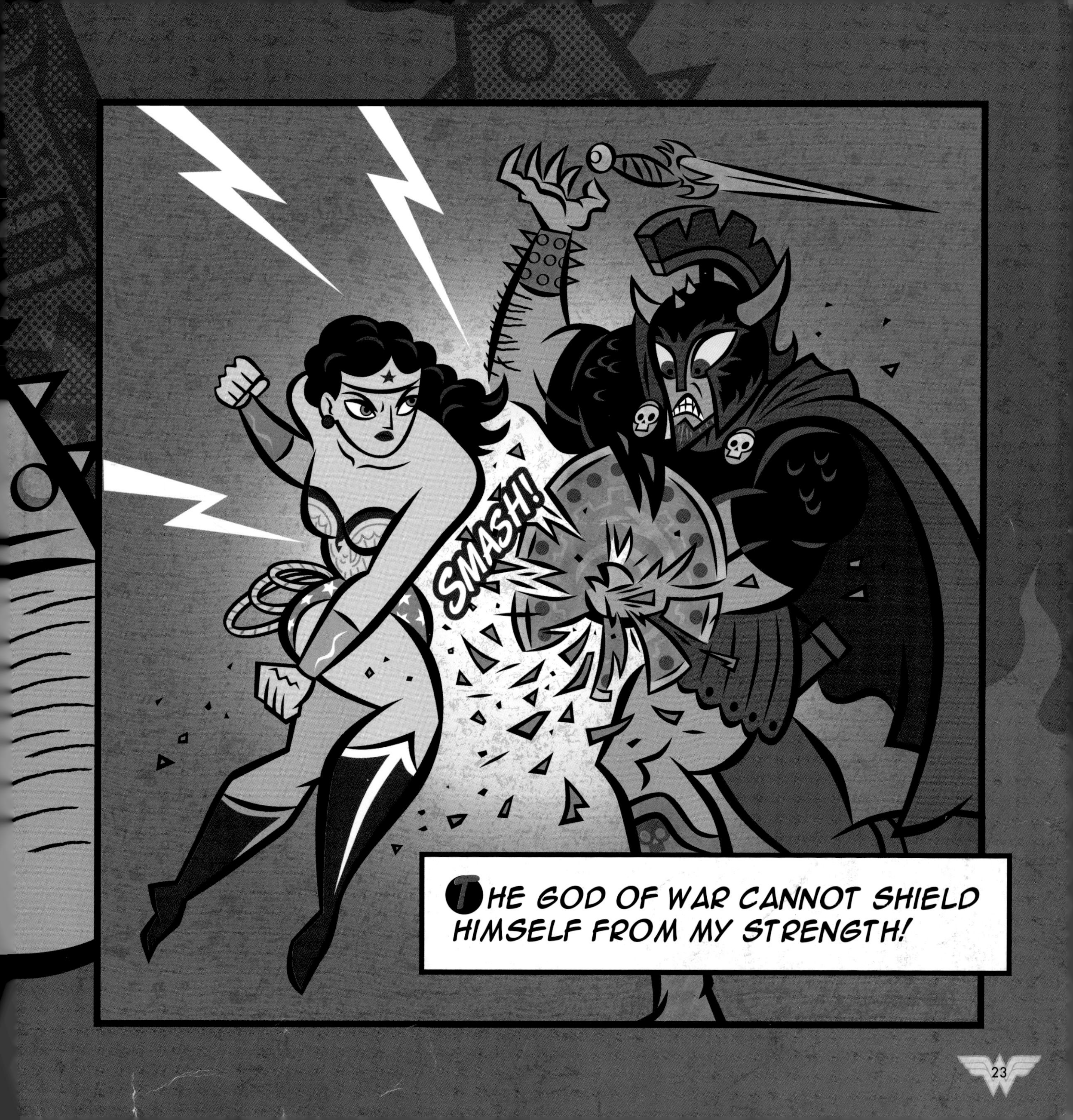
SMASH!
THE GOD OF WAR CANNOT SHIELD HIMSELF FROM MY STRENGTH!

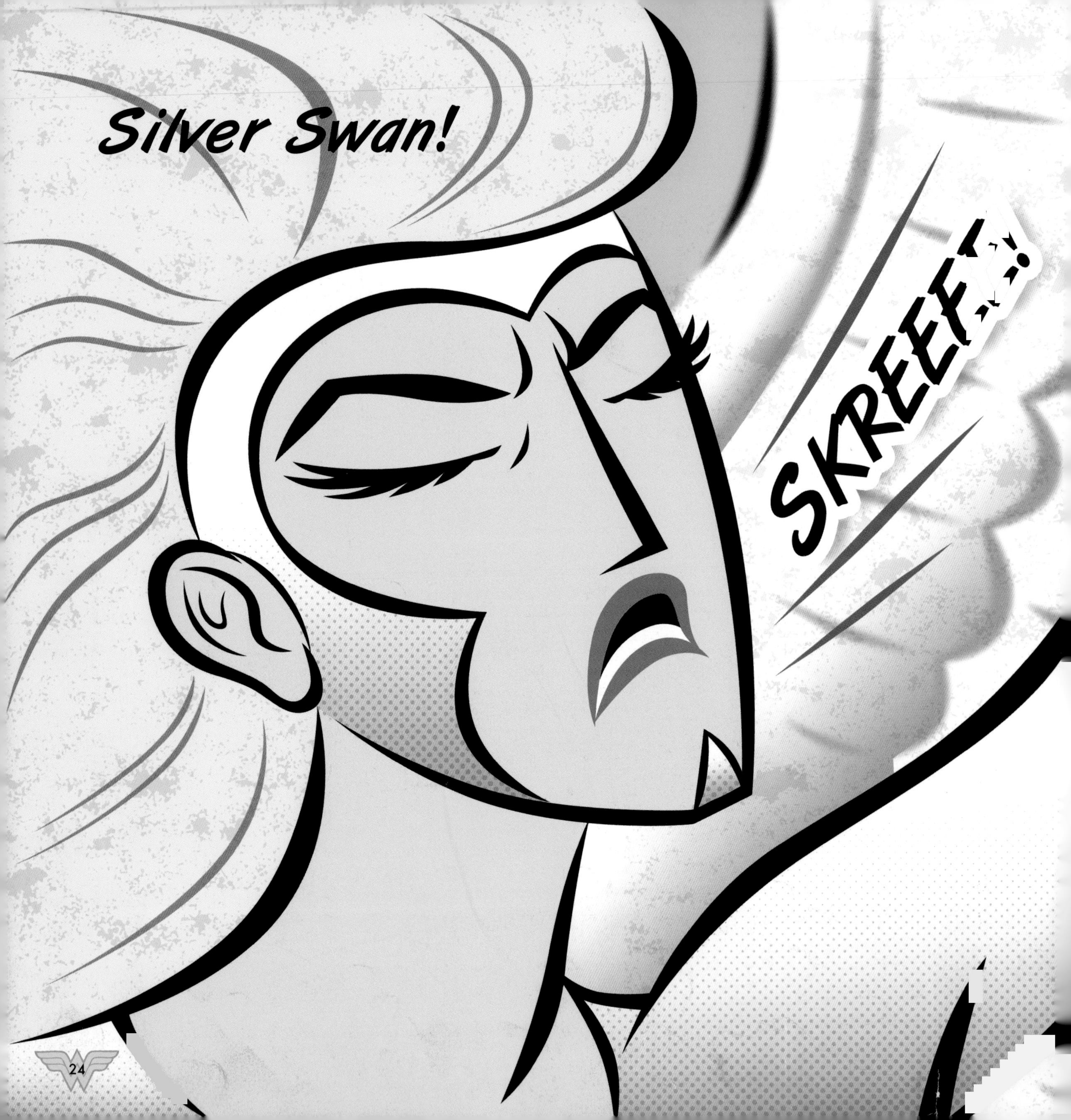
Silver Swan!
SKREEE

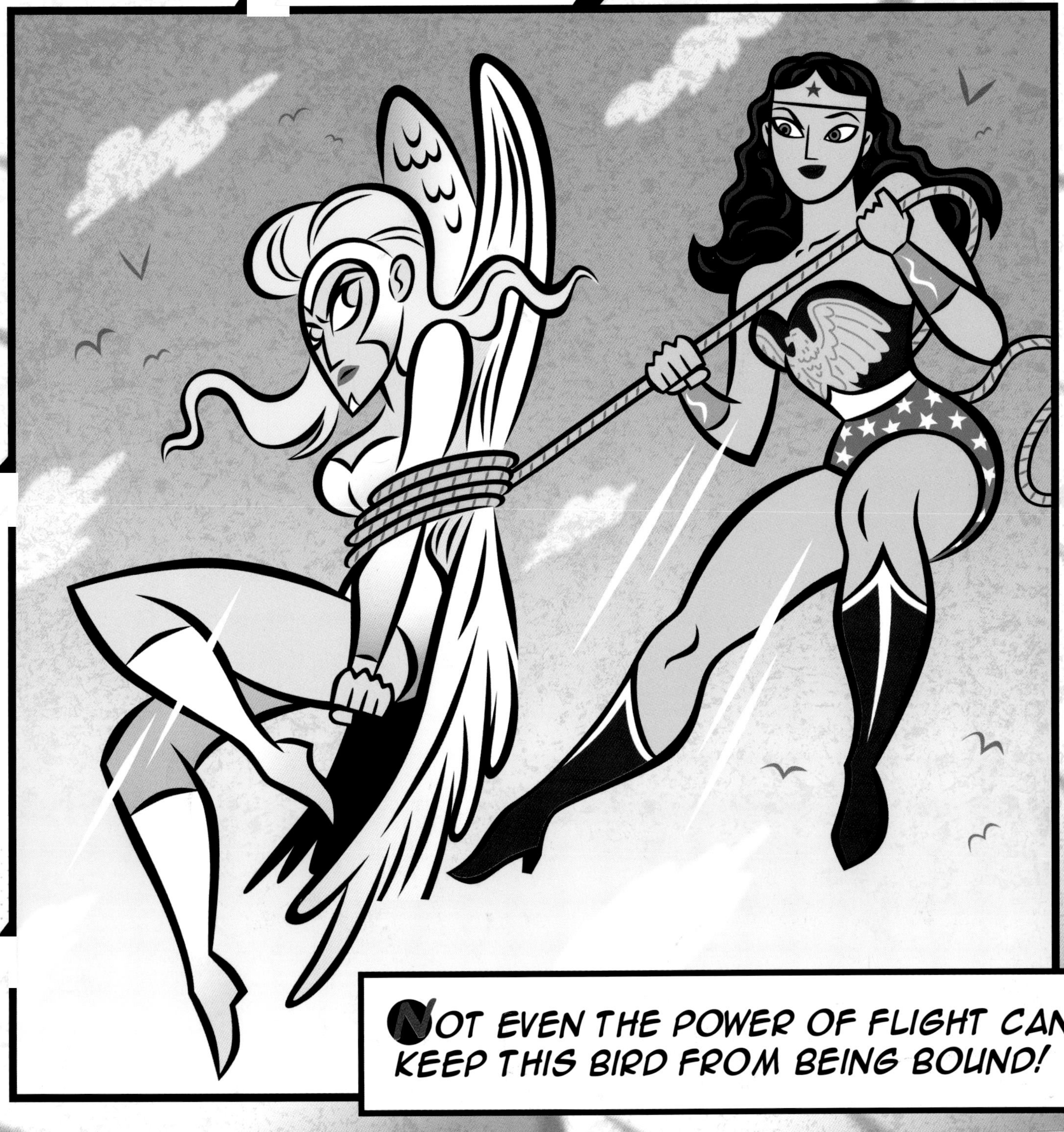
NOT EVEN THE POWER OF FLIGHT CAN KEEP THIS BIRD FROM BEING BOUND!

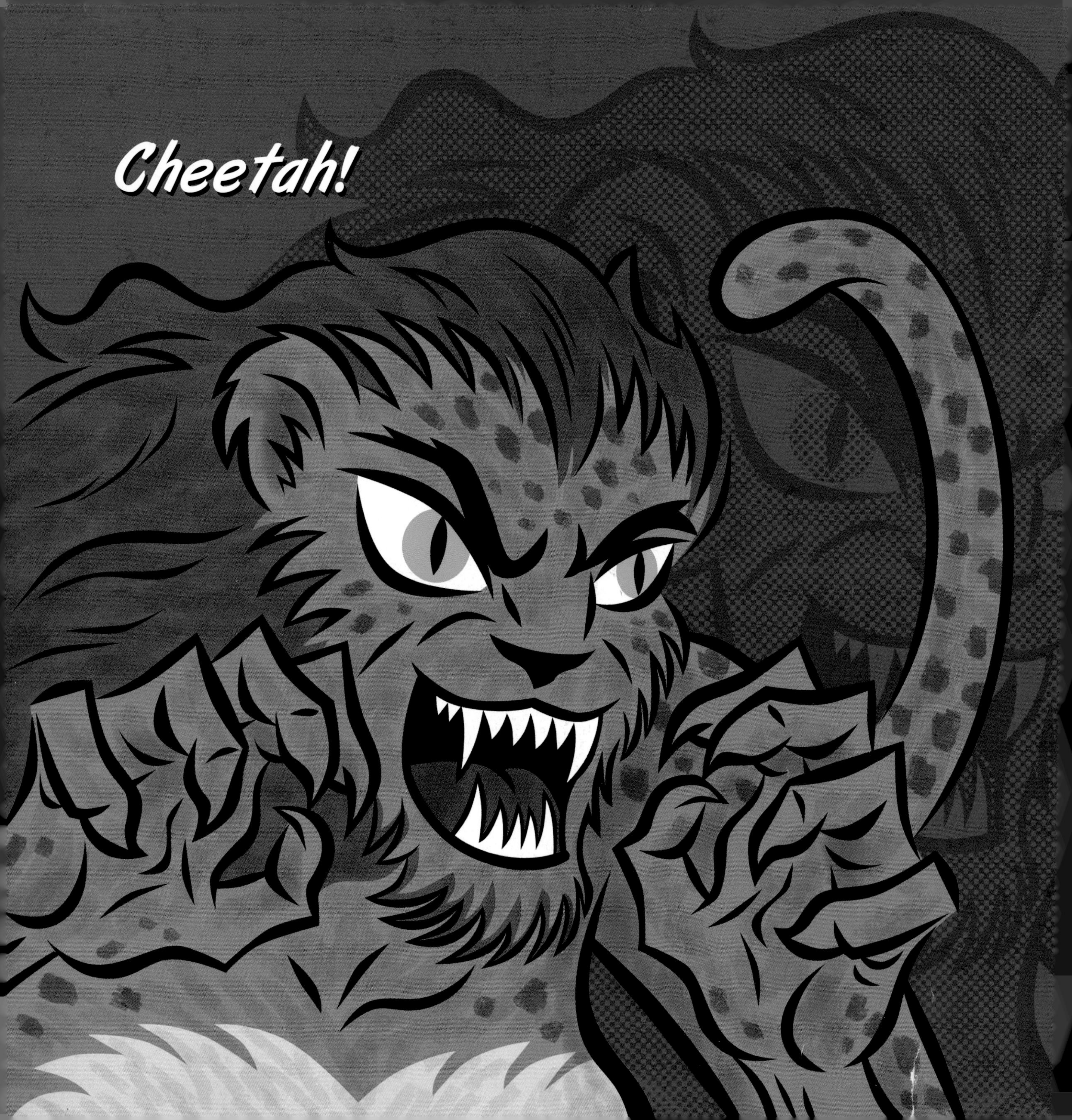
Cheetah!

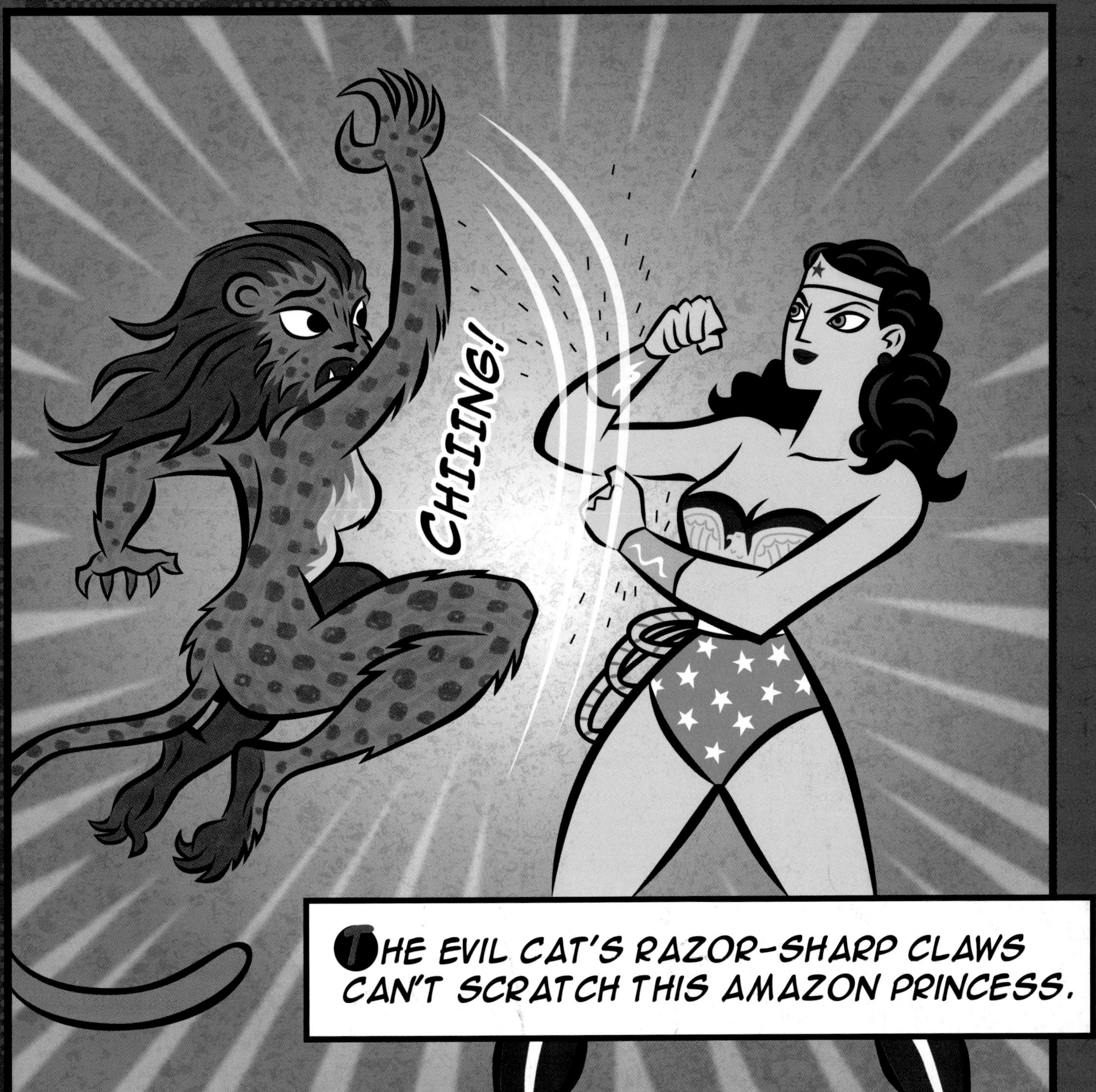
CHIIING!
THE EVIL CAT'S RAZOR-SHARP CLAWS CAN'T SCRATCH THIS AMAZON PRINCESS.

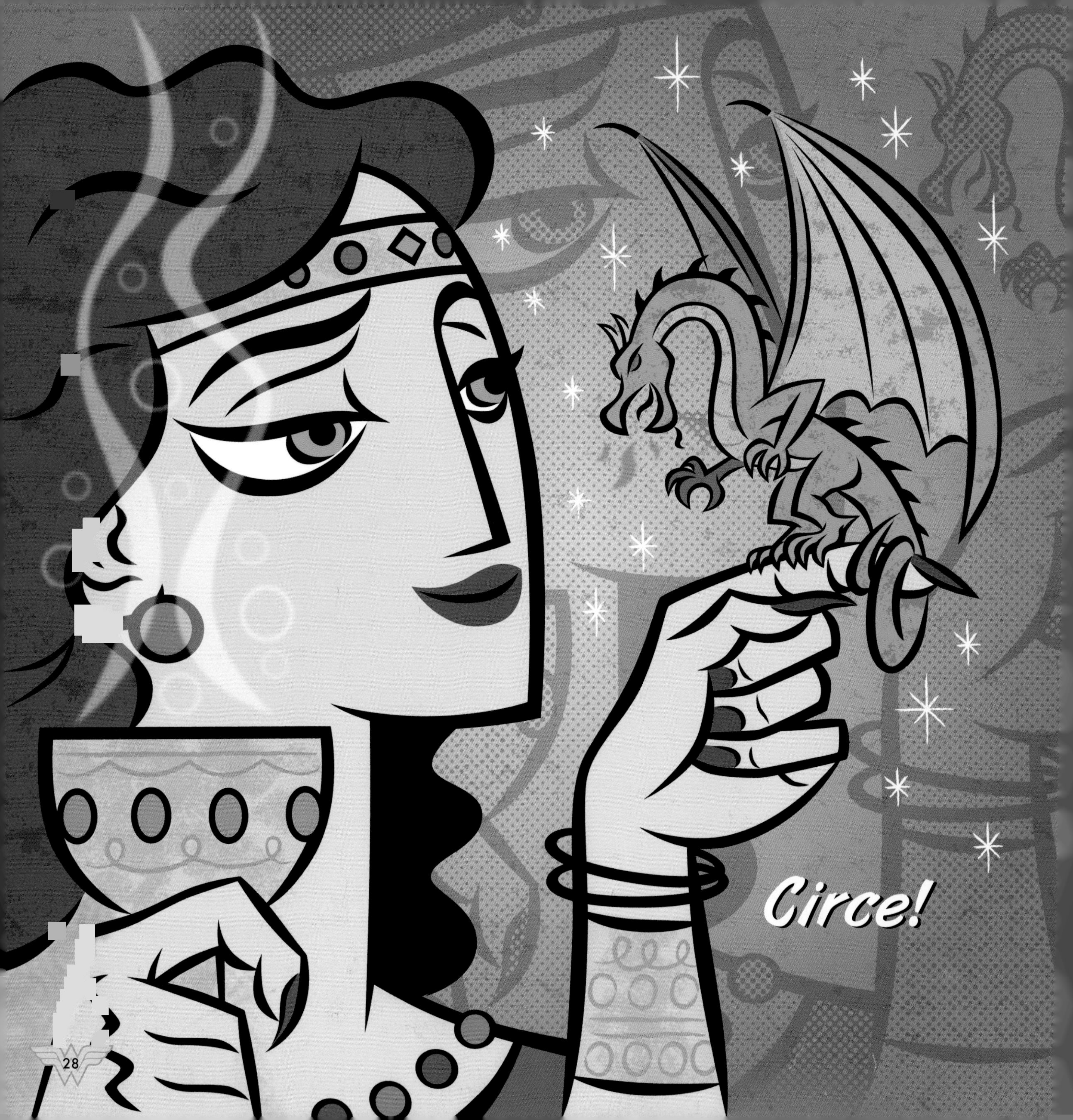
Circe!

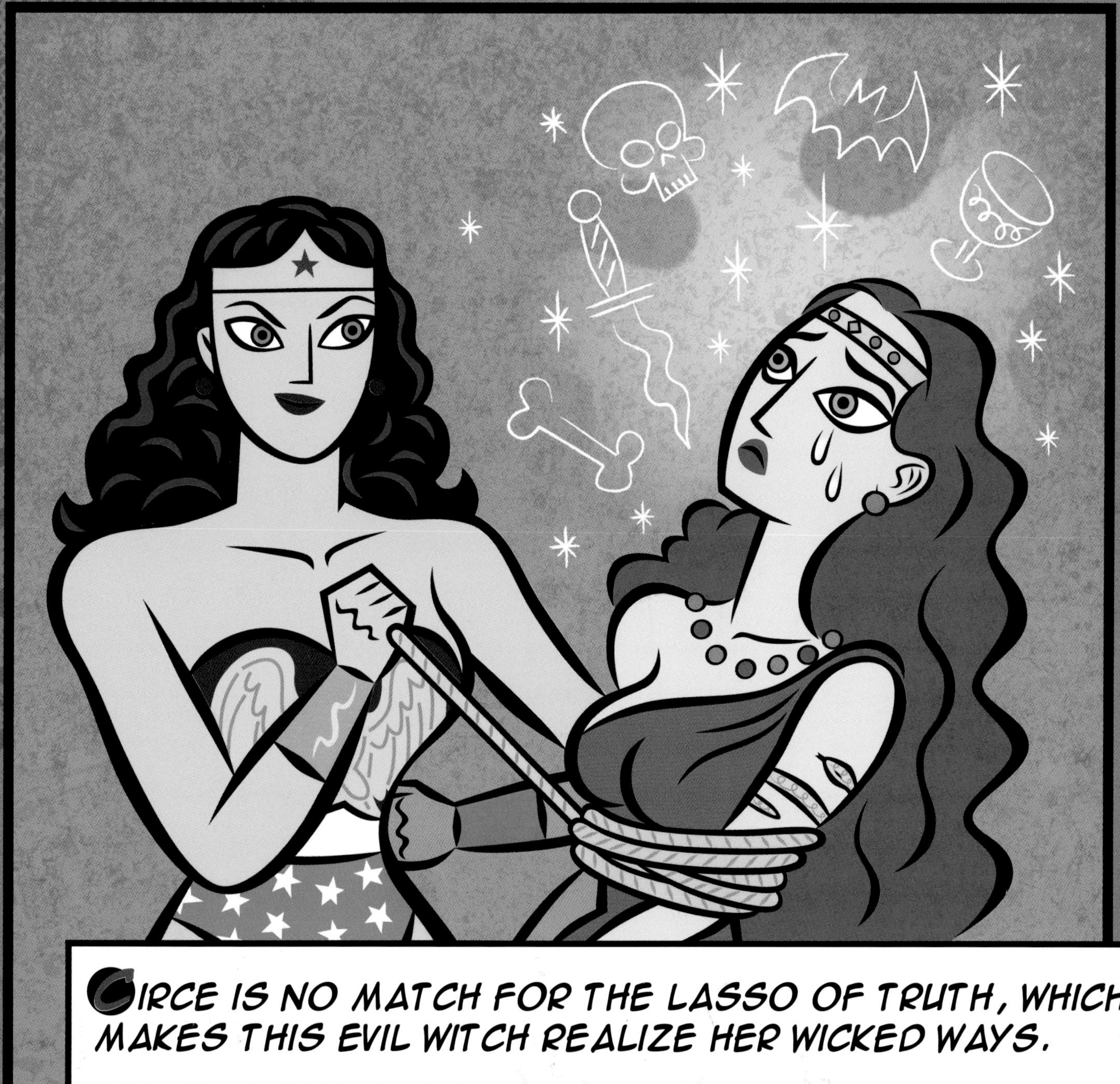
CIRCE IS NO MATCH FOR THE LASSO OF TRUTH, WHICH MAKES THIS EVIL WITCH REALIZE HER WICKED WAYS.

MY MISSION IS TO TEACH PEACE AND RESPECT TO ALL . . .

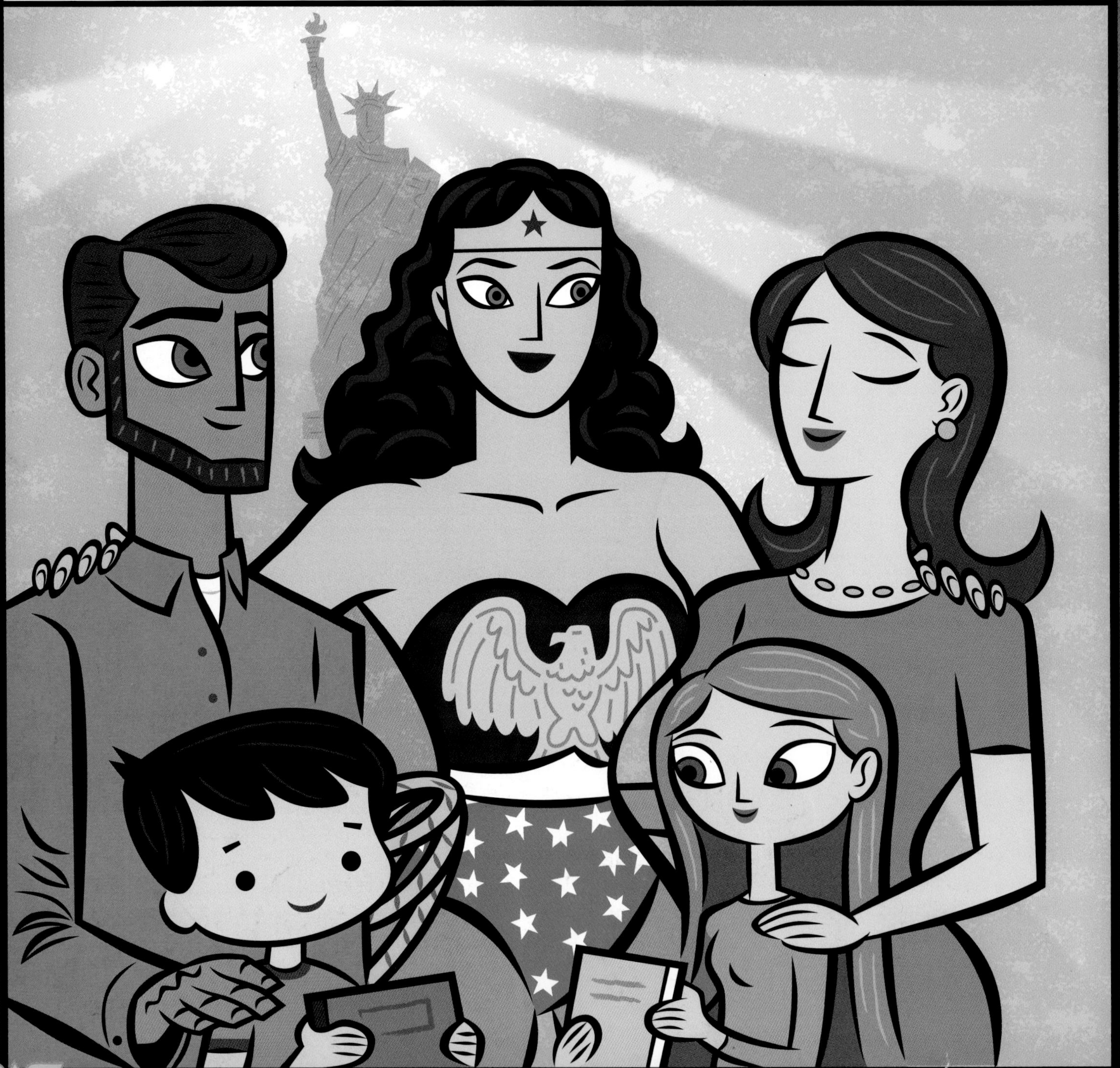

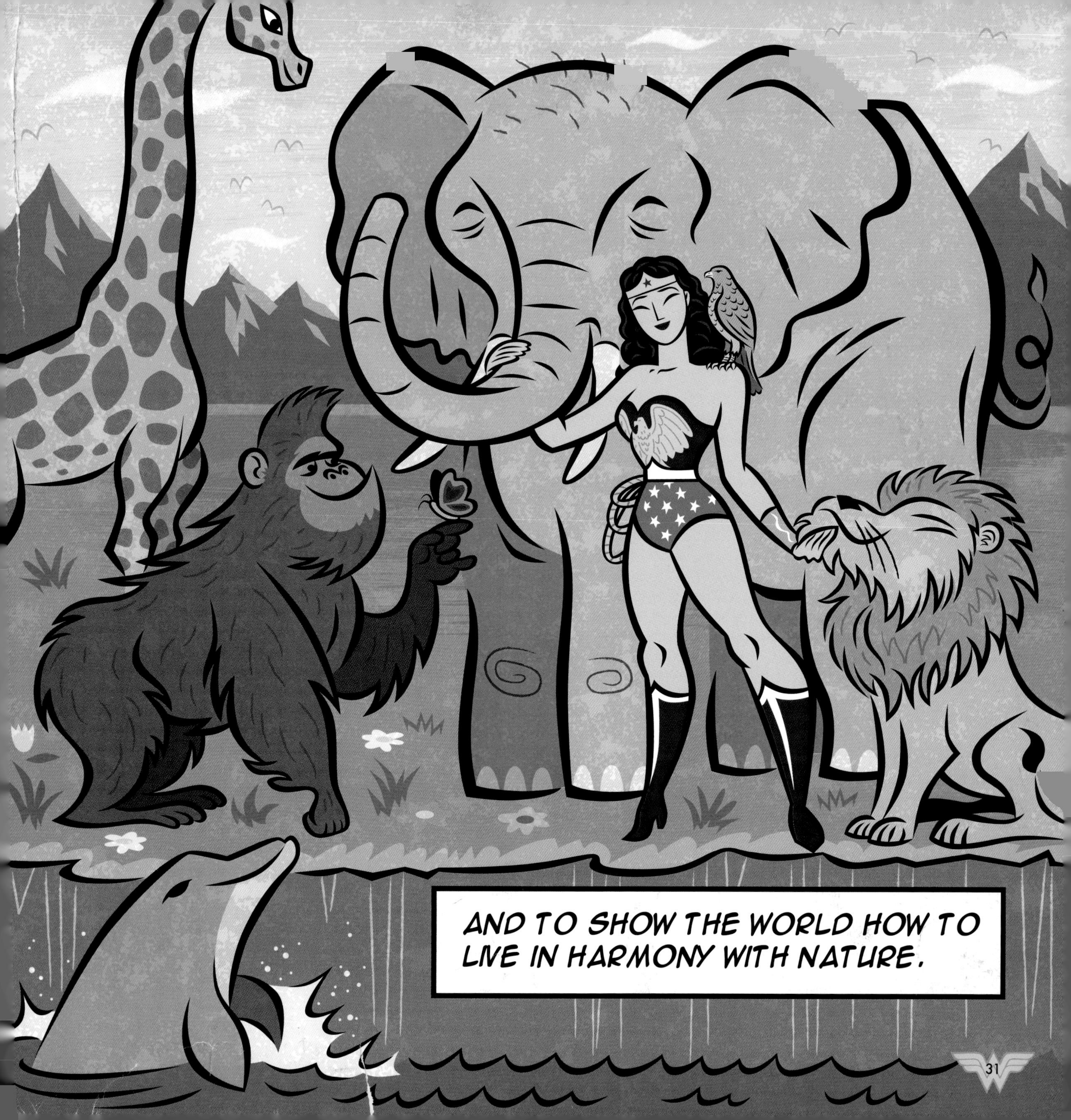
AND TO SHOW THE WORLD HOW TO LIVE IN HARMONY WITH NATURE.

I AM AN AMAZON PRINCESS, CHARGED TO SAVE MANKIND AND UNITE THE PEOPLE OF EARTH THROUGH LOVE AND KINDNESS.

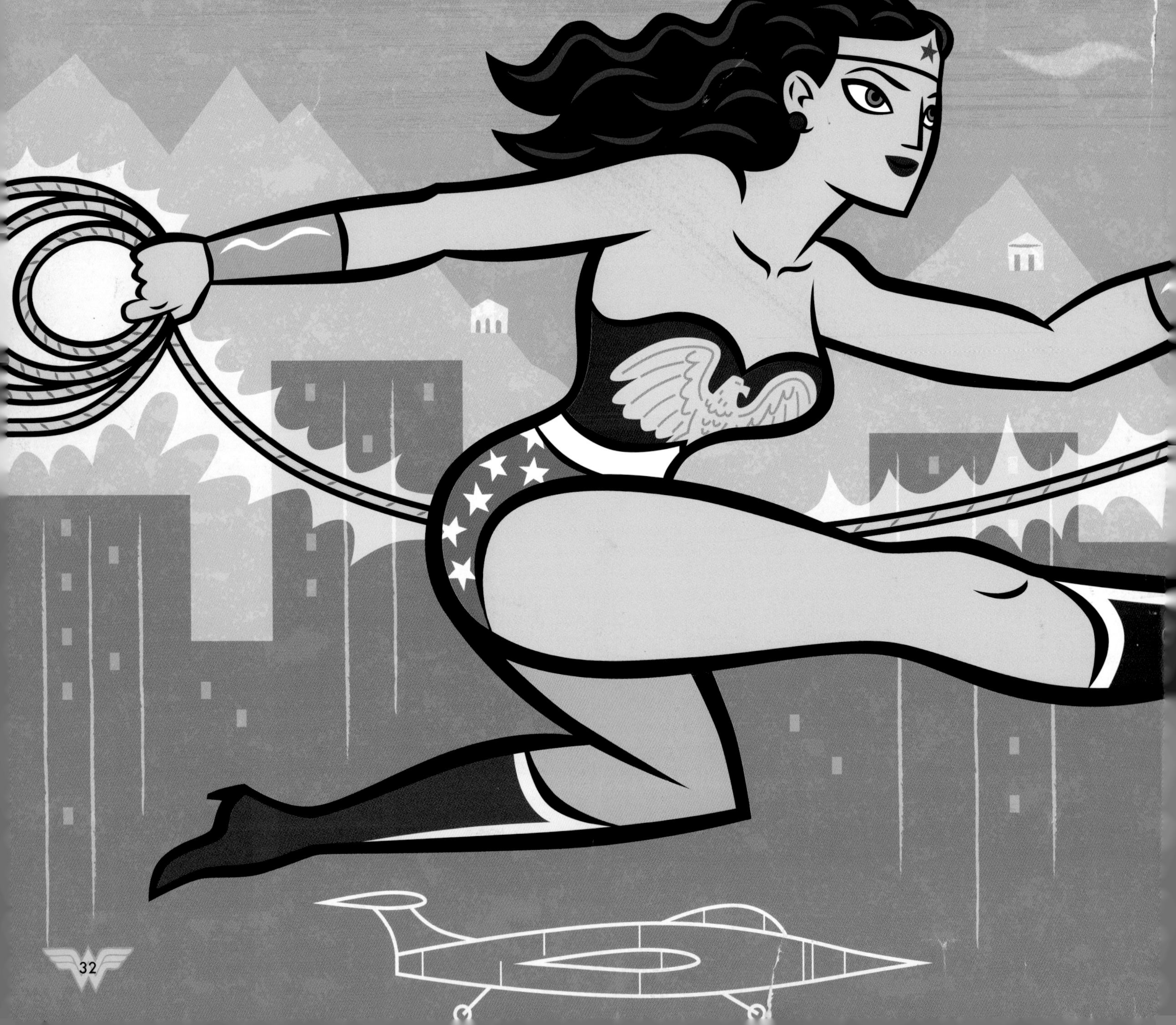

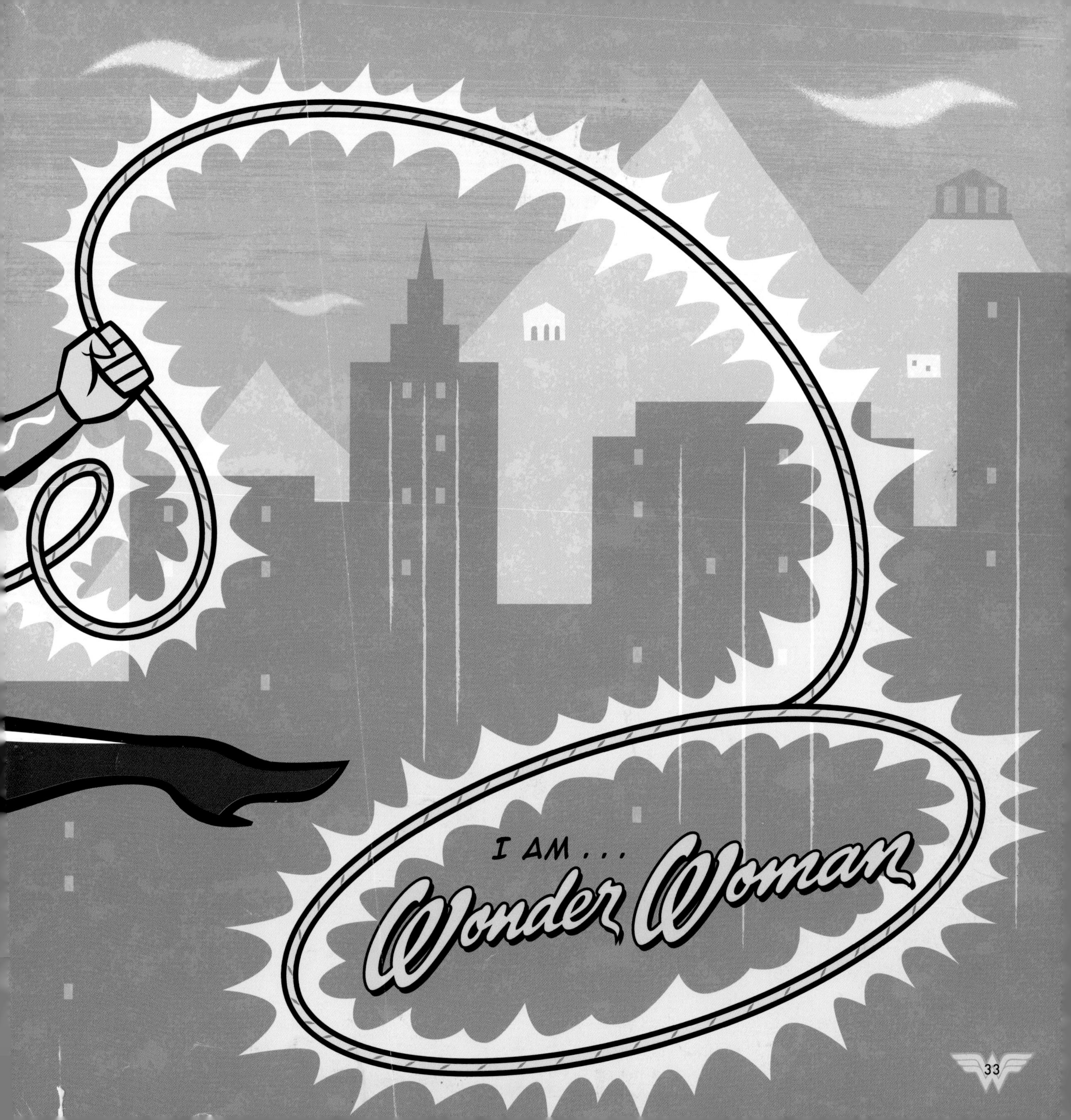
I AM . . .
Wonder Woman

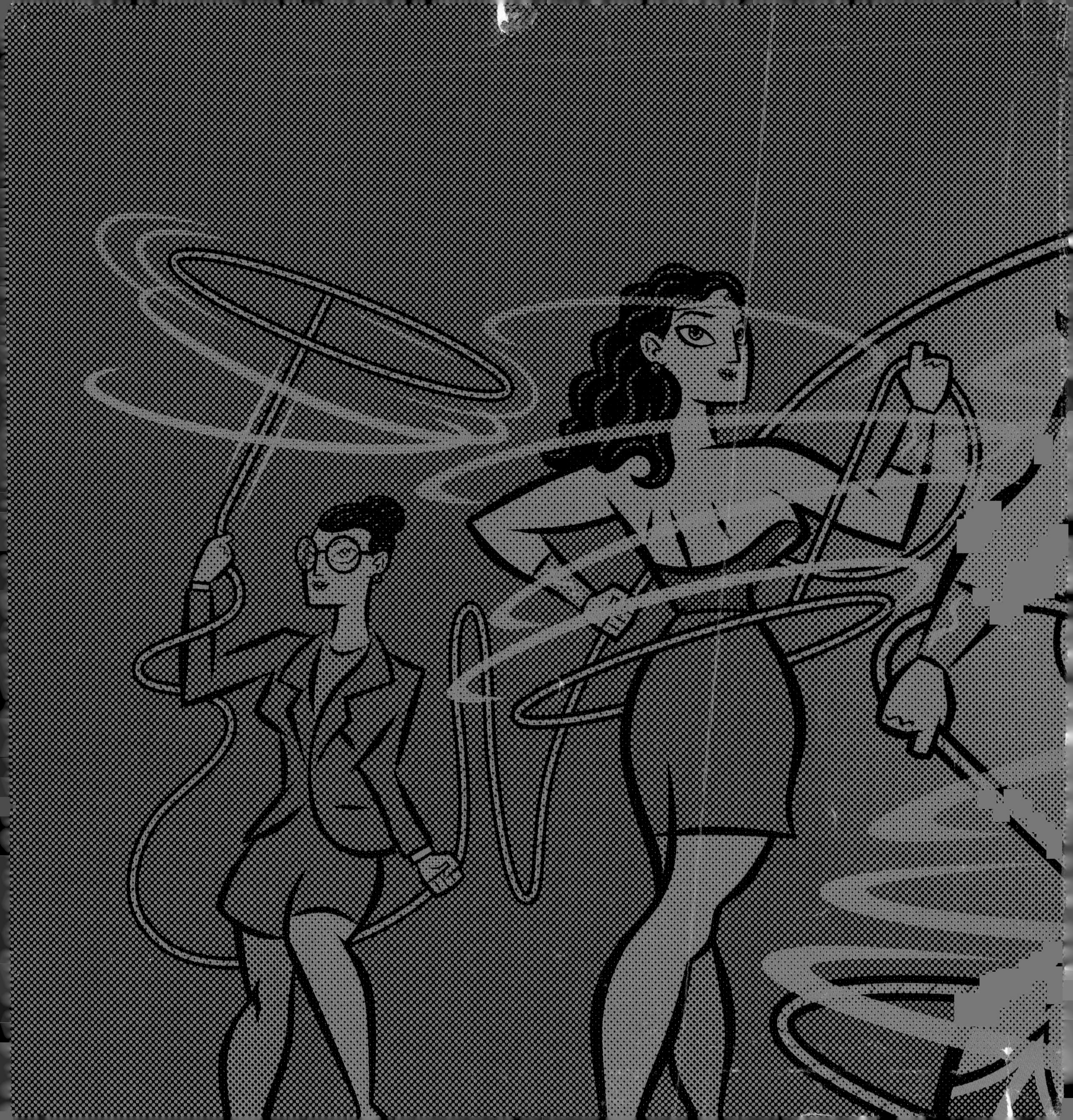